Cheaper to KEEP HER

PART 2

KS Publications
www.kikiswinson.net

Publisher's address:
K.S. Publications
P.O. Box 68878
Virginia Beach, VA 23471

Website: **www.kikiswinson.net**
Email: **KS.publications@yahoo.com**

ISBN-13: 978-0984529056
ISBN-10: 0-984529055

First Edition: May 2011
1098765

Editors: JWooden & Karen Johnson
Interior & Cover Design: Davida Baldwin (OddBalldsgn.com)
Cover Photography: Davida Baldwin (OBDPhotography.com)

Don't Miss Out On These Other Titles:

GET OUT OF JAIL FREE CARD

I was so happy to be out of jail.
But I was happier to know that Neeko's brother, Bishop, wanted Duke's head on a platter more than I did. I could see the rage in Katrina's eyes. She also wanted a piece of Duke. He was a man in desire and that desire was called death.

But I really wasn't trying to fuck with Katrina like that. After all the shit I went through with Diamond, I'd never trust another woman. Chicks were more grimy than niggas, so I knew I would deal with Bishop more so than her.

Katrina instructed the driver to drop everyone off at her place. I had no idea if she meant for me to get dropped off with her and Bishop, because she had not mentioned it to me. Hell, it didn't matter whatever plans she had up her sleeves for me, I was ready for anything, especially since I was no longer behind bars.

During the course of the drive I found myself staring out the side window. I looked at the cars that passed by us. I even glanced up at the birds in the sky and it felt really good to be able to see these things. Not only was I free in the physical, I was free in the mind. I'd always taken things for granted in the past, but now I've decided to take life more seriously and I vowed to never let another person take me out of my circle. My loyalty for others never meant shit to them, so now I'm going to do me. *I'm going to take care of Lynise.* And whoever has a problem with it, will just have to deal with it. I had one mission and that's to get what's due to me. And if I've got to die in the process, then so be it.

When the driver pulled up to Katrina's spot, he hopped out of the driver seat and rushed to open the door for her. One by one, we all filed out. First Katrina, exited the limo, followed by Bishop and then me. When I stood up on both feet, I looked at Bishop from head to toe. This guy was definitely easy on the eyes. He was every bit of six feet tall. Plus, I could tell he had a nice fit body underneath his blue Vintage bottom down shirt and his blue denim Rock & Republic jeans. The way he walked and carried himself reminded me of Denzel Washington.

I've always found older men more attractive than younger cats. In my experience, older men had a settled down mentality about them. While younger guys acted as if they had to jump from pillow to post. Bishop personified the quiet confidence of his generation and he was looking really good to me right now. I knew I was dead wrong for sizing him up like I was doing, especially since I had just gotten out of jail. And why was I in jail . . . because of the dirty work of my ex-lover, who also happened to be an older gentleman.

Damn, I have issues. That thought wasn't too far from the truth. I mean, you would think I had had enough of men who were ten to fifteen years my senior. But hell, I had just gotten out of jail and truthfully, I didn't know if I would spend my remaining years on earth in a six-by-six cell with bars. So I was in serious need of being held by somebody's man. Unfortunately for me, Katrina broke my train of thought by giving Bishop and me instructions on what to do next.

I stood next to Bishop and gave Katrina my undivided attention. As she began to speak, I couldn't help but take inventory of the lady. She was the average height of most women, around five-five, five-six, but she had the demeanor and intrinsic strength of a man. She wasn't masculine, that wasn't the strength she displayed. She was a woman who knew how to get from point A to point B in the blink of an eye. I could sense she had a hardheadedness about her. She was very attractive. It was easy to see why Neeko was so in love with her. She looked as if she was around my age. But she was a tiny little thing. There was no question in my mind that she weighed maybe a hundred and ten pounds soak and wet. She kind of reminded me of a thinner Meagan Good, except Meagan's long hair was real and Katrina was famous for sporting long and curly lace front wigs.

She looked directly at Bishop and said, "I have to call the funeral director back so we can finalize all the arrangements. So while I'm doing that why don't you take Lynise back to your hotel and wait for me to call you."

"How long you think that's gonna take you? Because remember I got some things to do myself and I also need to go out to the mall to pick out a suit."

"It won't take me long," Katrina said and then she looked down at her wristwatch. "It's almost noon, so give me until around five o'clock this evening to get back with you."

Bishop gave her a nod of approval. "All right. Five o'clock it is," he replied as he turned his attention towards me. "Come on, let's go," he instructed me.

I began to follow him towards an all-white late model Suburban, with New Jersey license plates. The windows were slightly tinted but he kept the rims factory. I jumped inside and sat down in the passenger seat. The smell of new leather filled the entire truck. I took in the new car smell and exhaled. And then I laid my head back against the headrest. I closed my eyes for a brief minute to soak in the moment.

Bishop cranked up the ignition and pulled away from Katrina's house. As he drove away my curiosity prompted me to open my eyes. I looked out the passenger side window at Katrina while she proceeded towards her house. Even though I frequent the Virginia Beach area, I had never been to this part of town. Initially, I hadn't noticed since I had sat in the back of the limo, but Katrina lived in a gated community. She and her neighbors' homes had to be in the neighborhood of at least a half million dollars or more. I knew Neeko had made a substantial amount of money at the club, but I had no idea he made the type of money to be able to afford this home. I mean, the club only had a packed house on Thursdays, Fridays and Saturdays. And even then, I still couldn't see him forking over six figures to maintain such an expensive residence.

If you asked me, he'd probably had some illegal shit going on like Duke. Since he was now six feet under, I would probably never know the real truth. Immediately after Katrina entered the house, I turned my attention towards Bishop. "Mind stopping by a fast food spot so I can get something to put on my stomach?" I asked.

"Sure. Where you wanna get something to eat from?" he replied.

I hunched my shoulders. "At this point I could care less," I told him.

I couldn't lie, my stomach felt as if it was in my back. Plus, I continued to hear my stomach growl so that was confirmation that I was on E. So if Bishop offered me a bowl of uncooked hotdogs I would have eaten it up in a matter of seconds. Fortunately for me, that didn't happen. After driving for only three miles, Bishop stopped by the Cheesecake Factory restaurant in the Pembroke area of Virginia Beach.

Immediately, an eerie feeling came over me. It started in my stomach. Duke and I used to frequent this very same restaurant when I lived in Duke's condo, which was located at the end of this block. All of the restaurant employees knew me. How could they not? Hell, I used order takeout at lease four times a week and on top of that, I used to tip well.

UNIQUE

That was my first concern. The second and more important concern was my appearance. I looked a hot damn mess with my hair braided back in fucking jailhouse cornrows. To bring it home, my face was bare and I knew I looked like shit without my make-up. Plus, the temperature was at least one hundred degrees outside and I had on the exact same velour sweat suit I was arrested in.

What am I gonna to do about this situation?

For one, I knew I couldn't play myself and go inside the restaurant because I was bound to be recognized. Two, I looked like an ex-con and to make matters worse, I even looked like some jailhouse chick's bitch. So to keep the whispering down to a minimum, I elected to stay inside Bishop's truck. I thought he would try to persuade me to do otherwise but he didn't. As a matter of fact, after I told him about my ties to this area, he decided to take me back to his hotel room and we would order pizza instead. I was okay by his decision to do that.

When he pulled up to the Hilton, which was only one block from the Cheesecake Factory and the exact same distance from the Cosmopolitan Building, I developed an eerie feeling in my stomach because I used to frequent this area when I lived in Duke's condominium. Bishop looked at me and said, "Don't worry. We're not gonna be here long."

Even after he told me we weren't going to be here long, I hesitated before I open the passenger side door. This area of Virginia Beach made me feel really uneasy. Duke was well known. People in this area knew him because he was a popular socialite. So the thought of running into him or someone who knew him or our history was kind of getting to me.

I was concerned and in my mind I wondered if I was overreacting. This man, Bishop, seemed as if he wouldn't let anything happen to me. But my concern focused on knowing how sinister Duke was. Additionally, I knew how coldhearted the men who worked for him was. Then it hit me, or I should say something inside of me connected the dots and convinced that I'd be all right. After all, I was with this man called Bishop.

After a couple of minutes of much thought, I let my guard down and stepped outside of the truck. Bishop escorted me inside of the hotel lobby and then he led me onto the elevator. The elevator took us to the fifth floor. Bishop's room was only a couple doors down from the elevator. He stuck his key card inside the lock and let us both inside. I took a seat on the sofa next to the bed and watched as Bishop picked up the remote control. He handed it to me after he pressed the power button.

"Here. Turn it to whatever you want to watch while I order the pizza."

"Okay," I responded and took the remote. I pressed down on the channel button and sifted through the channels until I came across a re-run of the Jamie Fox show, which was my favorite show. I tuned into the show to take my mind off everything that was going on in my life. Unfortunately, that was short lived when I heard a knock at the hotel room's door. I nearly jumped out of my seat. Bishop looked at me like I had lost my damn mind.

"It's okay. I'm sure it's just the pizza delivery guy," he assured me.

UNIQUE

I exhaled. *Breathe. I have to breathe.* I was still somewhat leery until he opened the door and I heard the conversation that transpired between him and the pizza delivery guy. Once Bishop paid him, the guy thanked Bishop and left. The moment the door closed, it felt as if a huge load was lifted from my shoulders. I swear, being in this area of Virginia Beach spooked the hell out of me. If I had things my way, I wouldn't be here at all. I would be knocking on the front door of my ex-boy friend, Devin. And he'd love it too. He'd relish in the moment of me having to crawl back to him and beg him to let me come back to live with him.

Beside Diamond's grimy ass, I had nobody else I could go to for help. So he would had eaten this shit up! Now I can't say what's gonna happen with me, Bishop and Katrina. But whatever they had in mind, I needed to be included in on it, because at this point, I didn't have a penny to my name or a place I could call my own. And before we departed ways, I was gonna have to come up with a solid plan to get back on my grind. And whether Bishop and Katrina knew it or not, they were going to be the ones to help me.

I was the third member of their Musketeer act.

Playing Mind Games

I *devoured a couple slices of pizza while I watched rerun after rerun of Jamie's old show.*

Bishop took off his shoes and sat back on the bed with his back pressed against the headboard. He started off making small talk during commercial breaks between the shows but then the seriousness of the conversation picked up. And for the first time in my life I was at a lost for words. "Are you ready to help me bury that cock sucking nigga for what he did to my brother?" he asked.

Even the anger in his voice came out smooth and unpretentious. Before I answered Bishop, I looked into his eyes and saw the pain he had buried in his heart. I had no clue how close Neeko and Bishop were, but I knew that they were blood related and that was enough to avenge his brother's death. I tried to avoid answering his question, but it didn't work. Bishop continued to press the issue.

"I swear, I can't wait until I get my motherfucking hands on that piece of fucking shit! I'm going to take his fucking head off and feed it to a couple of stray dogs!" he continued to bark. I knew his bite was far worse than his bark. I literally saw steam coming from his nostrils like he was a raging bull. This guy was beyond livid and so was I but I remained quiet. I figured the hurt that I had suffered at the hands of Duke would be vindicated sooner than later. And I'd be very grateful when it was all said and done.

Just being around Bishop was intense and over-whelming on a level I couldn't describe. He was danger, trouble and destruction rolled up in a lean package. I hadn't seen the man in action but something told me his reputation was well-deserved.

After Bishop had calmed down from his ranting, he came out of left field and asked me what kind of deal had I worked up with the police? He totally caught me off guard with the question. I didn't know whether to be honest with him and tell him I agreed to work with the police or lie and act like I was some ride or die chick and I walked out of jail because my lawyer worked a miracle for me. Bishop came across as a no nonsense type of cat that took the law into his own hands. But then again, I could've read him wrong. So to test the waters, I took a death breath and told him what I thought he'd want to hear.

"I don't fuck with the police like that. They're the ones who locked me up," I began to explain. "I had some court appointed attorney who actually did his homework and realized that the state didn't have shit on me. All that bogus ass evidence they thought they had wasn't worth shit. So the judge let me go free."

"How long were you in jail?"

"A couple of weeks."

"That wasn't very long," he commented and then he sat straight up in the bed. He looked as if he was about to stand but when he lifted his butt up from the bed and tugged on the hem of his shirt, I let out a sigh of relief. I mean, I was in this state of mind that I couldn't trust anybody. Especially after all the shit I've been through. Because of motherfuckers I thought I could trust . . . and one nasty bitch I thought I could trust. But from this day forward, I was going to start looking out for Lynise since everybody seemed as if they were out for themselves.

I cleared my throat and then I said, "It may not have been long to you but it seemed like forever for me."

Bishop smiled at me. But it wasn't the kind of smile you'd see on a picture. It was a sneaky looking kind of smile. "Think you could do some hard time?" he asked me.

Once again this nigga came out of left field with another crazy ass question. I knew this was another test to see if I could be trusted and was I the type of woman who'd hold my own in the heat of the moment. Now I wanted to clown his ass and turn the question back on him so he could answer it. But again, I held my tongue and told him some shit he wanted to hear.

"The only way I'd do some hard time is if somebody did something to me or somebody I love and I had to kill their motherfucking ass! So, to answer your question, yes, I'd gladly sit my ass down in a cell behind protecting and defending something or someone I love."

UNIQUE

Bishop sat there and listened to my response but he didn't flinch. He acted as if he wasn't impressed by one word I said. So my mind was running around in circles trying to read his facial expression. Finally, he said, "Let's say you and your man were in a car together and a cop pulled you over, would you take the charge if he told you that there was a gun inside the glove compartment?"

I knew the clock was ticking after Bishop asked me that dumb ass question. I wanted so badly to tell him hell nah! I wouldn't take a charge for my own mother! So he needed to back the fuck up. But for the third and final time, I fed him a dumb ass answer and prayed that our Q and A session was over. "He wouldn't have to ask me to take the charge for him, especially if he's already been to jail or was out on parole or something. Better yet, I would still take the gun charge because I know how judges are more lenient with women than men." I sat straight up on the sofa as if I was the shit because I knew I had said some good shit. I knew I fucked Bishop up with that answer. He wasn't ready for me. But little did he know, I was lying my ass off. Shit! If he jaywalked across the fucking boulevard and the cops asked me who he was, I would give his name up in a heartbeat. He didn't mean shit to me in no way, form, shape or fashion. And that's the way I intended to keep it.

I assumed Bishop bought my answer because he seemed a little more relaxed now than he did when we started the conversation. If he were one of those people who could read a person's body language and could detect if they were lying or not, he would have failed miserably. I called him a dummy underneath my breath and then I turned my attention back towards the TV. Apparently he wasn't done speaking to me because he chimed right back, "You know I'm going to need you to bring Duke to me right?"

For a moment there it seemed like Bishop spoke a different language. I mean, I heard him quite clearly but I couldn't quite wrap my thoughts around his question. *Is he on drugs or something? Does he think I was stupid enough to let him use me as bait?* Duke was a very dangerous man and he had a lot of insane men that worked for him. *Does he think that I would risk my life to serve Duke on a platter to him?* Okay, granted Duke railroaded me and had me arrested for some shit I had nothing to do with, which is enough to kill him over. And Duke also made the call to have Neeko killed so I kind of felt sorry for Bishop, but I realized in jail that I was there all by my lonesome. No one came to my rescue so I figured that my best bet was to stay in my own lane because at this point he couldn't provide me a safe house like the police could. So I wasn't about to make any deals with him. No way.

"I take it you're not feeling what I'm saying right now," he commented.

"It's not that," I began to lie. "I'm just trying to gather my thoughts. I mean, I just got out of jail for something I didn't have a thing to do with. So, you know I'm angry as hell. But I figure if I'm going to make Duke pay for all the shit he's taken me through, then I'm going to have to play my cards right. I can't afford to fuck up like I did the last time."

"Why don't you let me do all the thinking, then we'll both come out on top."

"The last time I let someone else do the thinking for me, I got crossed up. I can't let that happen again." I stood my ground. But Bishop possessed this air of influence. He even looked convincing to the point where I wanted to believe that he'd handle my situation. But then I figured that the last time I judged a book by its cover I got railroaded. So I had to be strong-minded with the notion that it was best to keep myself guarded. This world we lived in was cold and infested with heartless people. No one gave a fuck about Lynise. Not even my family or Diamond, whom I thought was my best friend. With the way things were looking right now, I figured I could pretend as if I was down with all that rah-rah bullshit Bishop was talking, but I was going to do things my own way. It's about Lynise now. Fuck the world and everything on it.

I allowed to Bishop to layout his plan for Duke. I could tell he wanted Duke dead but he was very careful about saying the actual words. All he kept saying was that he wanted Duke to pay for Neeko's murder. And then he sketched out a scenario about how he'd love to catch Duke coming out of his house late at night and kidnap his ass. He didn't say exactly what he'd do to him but when I looked in Bishop's eyes, I could see death as clear as day. I knew then that once he got his hands on Duke, that Duke would die very slowly. The thought of it was like music to my ears.

After Bishop said what he had to say, he got up from the bed and stepped out of the hotel room. When the door closed behind him I sat there and became very suspicious. I mean, he didn't utter a word about what he was about to do. He had just gotten up and literally walked out of the room. I had gotten paranoid for a second, but when I heard his voice, I knew he stepped out of the room to make a call. Without hesitation, I eased up from where I was sitting and tiptoed to the door so I could hear his conversation. When I reached the door I placed my right ear against it. I held my breath because in my mind I felt as if I was making a lot of noise and I didn't want to bring any unwarranted attention to myself.

"Did you make the call like I asked you to do earlier?" I heard him say to whoever was on the other end of the phone.

"What did he say?" his questions continued. "Nah, tell him he's gonna have to do better than that. I got a lot riding on this and I ain't gonna let nobody fuck that up for me. So call him back and tell him I said that if he ain't going to come correct then there's nothing else to say." He stopped talking and everything went silent. I could hear the frustration in his tone. He was not at all happy about whatever he was discussing. I figured if he found me standing next to the door eavesdropping on his phone call, then who knows what he would have done to me. I wasn't about to find out how powerful his wrath was. So I eased my way back from the door and sat my nosy ass back down on the chair. Thank God for a woman's intuition because as soon as I sat back down he grabbed a hold of the doorknob and opened the door.

He looked directly at me as he held his Blackberry pressed against his ear. The way he stared at me made me feel uneasy. I guess he sensed that I might have been eavesdropping on his conversation, but when he noticed I was sitting in the same spot he backed himself back out the door and closed it.

Right after he closed the door, I let out a long sigh. And I thanked my lucky stars that I went with my first gut to sit my ass back down. If I hadn't, I couldn't tell you what he would've said or done.

Before he reentered the room I heard him tell the caller that he wanted to hear from them by the end of the day. Then he said, "And if you ain't got my money right by the time I get back there then you're going to have some problems too."

Immediately after, the door opened while he simultaneously stuffed his phone into his front pocket. I didn't say one word to him. I pretended as if he wasn't there and continued to look at TV. He took a seat back on the bed. I could still see him staring at me though my peripheral vision. I started to ask him if there was a problem, but I decided against it for fear he might say something I didn't want to hear. So I damn near bit my tongue to keep me from opening my mouth. But finally he said something, so I was able to let go of the urge.

"How well do you know Katrina?" he asked.

I was thrown for a loop when he asked me that question. I mean, why would he ask me something like that? I really didn't know Katrina at all. She hardly ever showed up at the club. She was more behind the scenes. Now we knew she was in the picture, she just wouldn't make herself seen. So, I turned towards him and told him the truth. And after I told him how she'd only come to the club maybe once or twice a month, he gave me a weird look.

"What would she be doing when she did come around?" he questioned.

"Nothing unusual. She would take inventory of the liquor and beer, check the sales tape from my register and then she'd go back to the back office where Neeko was."

"Have you ever seen her steal money from him?" he blurted out. I swear I had no idea he was about to throw that power ball at me. And I really didn't expect for him to give me that sinister look either. I was starting to feel uncomfortable all over again. But I held on to my cool and pretended I could handle whatever he threw my way.

"No, I've never seen her take anything from him. I mean, if she did, she must've done it while she was in his office. But out in the opening where everybody could see her, nope, I didn't see her lift a finger."

Bishop looked away from me and focused his attention on the TV. I knew he wasn't interested in the show that was airing because his body language spoke volumes. Two minutes later, he turned his attention back to me. I thought at one point he was about to say something but his mouth didn't open. I felt uncomfortable with him sitting there looking at me and had nothing to say. So I got up the gumption to say something on my own. I had to clear the air if nothing else. "Are you okay?" I asked.

"Don't I look okay?" he reserved the question.

I thought for a second because I heard the sarcasm reeking from his tone. I had no idea where this conversation was going but I knew it was going somewhere. If I wanted to stay on his good side then I felt it would be best to handle him with kid gloves.

"You appear to be fine. But I could be wrong," I replied and then I hunched my shoulders. I didn't want to come across to Bishop that I was some smartass chick with a chip on her shoulders. I knew I was in his world. And I knew I couldn't call any shots. So I did what any woman would do in a situation like mine: I kissed his ass and got what I could get while the getting was good.

"Look Lynise, I'm gonna be straight up with you. I came here to help bury my brother, Neeko. Now I know who put the hit out on my brother, but I need to know who fired the shot that killed him and I need to find out what's going on with Katrina."

Surprised by his comment, I said, "I'm confused. What's wrong with Katrina?"

Bishop took a deep breath and said, "I've had a chance to look at the books from the club and the numbers are off like a muthafucka!"

"Did you approach her with it?"

"Yeah, I did. But she's not giving me the answers that I need."

I shook my head in disbelief and said, "Now I can't tell you who actually killed Neeko because I was behind bars. And I can't tell you if I saw Katrina stealing money from the club. But I will say that I heard Neeko fussing a few times about money was coming up short."

"Who was he talking to when he said that?"

"He was talking to Katrina. But she brushed him off and told him he needed to stop drinking so much because it's messing with his head. And that's about it."

Bishop fell silent once again. I wished I had more information for him but I didn't. I honestly never saw Katrina take anything from the club. And if she did, she damn sure did a hell of a job hiding it. "So, how do you plan to find out if she was stealing money from him?" I asked.

"Don't worry because I've got it all figured out."

The coldness in his tone gave me the chills all over.

MY PUSSY IS ALL I GOT

*O*ne hour passed while Bishop and I sat in the hotel room and watched TV.

I grew tired of sitting around and wanted to take a shower. I wanted so badly to get out of my clothes but not having a change of clothing posed a problem. So I looked at Bishop and asked him if he'd lend me a few dollars so I could run across the street to Pembroke Mall to get a few things. "How much do you think you'll need?" he asked me.

I thought for a second but I couldn't come to an appropriate amount to ask him for. I'd only known him for about two hours so for me to ask him for a specific dollar amount would be insane. I told him I didn't know. Then I said, "Why don't you walk with me over to the mall. That way I could pick out what I need and then you could pay for it."

Bishop smiled at me and his response was, "And what am I going to get in return?"

"What do you mean by that?" I blurted. Was he insinuating that I fuck him for the things I needed from the mall? I mean, if that's what he wanted, then he'd have to do more than just buy me a pair of panties with a fucking shirt and pair of pants. He'd have to put me in a fucking house like Duke's slimy ass did. And he'd have to put me in something better than that BMW X6 I was driving too. I know I haven't always lived in an upscale apartment building with a doorman and wore all the latest labels, but I did have a chance to experience it. So I couldn't accept anything else.

Finally, Bishop smiled at me and said, "I'm just pulling your leg, sweetheart. Come on, let's go. I need to go over there to pick up a pair of black dress socks."

Instead of saying something sassy to him, I smiled and then I stood to my feet. He stood up right after I did and retrieved the hotel key card from the TV stand. I opened the door of the room and then we both made our exit.

Pembroke Mall was directly across the street from the hotel so it took us approximately five minutes to get there. We made small talk along the way. "Have you ever shopped at this mall?" he started off.

"Not really. The only time I'd come over here was to get take-out from the food court or to pay my cell phone bill at the kiosk. This mall is geared towards young white kids who like to wear that skateboard clothing. They got plenty of white people clothing stores in here. That's why black people either go to Lynnhaven Mall or Military Circle Mall."

"Well, if they only have white people stores at this mall then why are we coming here?"

"They got a department store inside the mall called Kohl's, so I should be able to find me something present-able. I mean, all I need is something to change into after I take me a long hot shower. It could be a ten-dollar sun-dress for all I care. My main concern is to get out of these clothes I got on my back now. The label on the inside of the clothes don't matter to me at this point."

Bishop smiled at me once again and then he reached for the door to enter the mall and opened it.

Right after we entered into the mall we stopped inside of the store called Legends. Legends catered to both black and white people, so I knew I'd fine something ei-ther way I looked at it. I sifted through the clothes on the rack while Bishop's phone began to ring. He took it from the holster and then he looked at the caller ID screen. "It's Katrina," he said to me and answered, "Hello."

He stepped away from me and headed to the entrance of the store. I realized he wanted some privacy so I turned my back to him and pretended to mind my business. I couldn't hear every word he uttered but I heard enough to know he was getting irritated with her.

"But I thought that they were only charging you ten grand," he said. I wish I could hear what Katrina was say-ing in return. "So, why are they asking you for another five grand?" he asked and then he waited for Katrina to respond. "Look Katrina, I understand all of that, but at the end of the day they're pouring salt in the fucking game. And I don't like being played." His conversation continued. "I'm going to need to see something in black and white before I shell out another dime. Neeko had a life insurance policy with Lincoln Life, so that's who you need to be calling." And right after he uttered those last few words, he ended his call.

I acted as if I hadn't heard bits and pieces of his conversation by pretending to search through the clothes on the racks. He approached me from behind. "I can't wait to get through this week so I can head back up north," he said.

I looked back at him. "I take it you just got rubbed the wrong way."

"You don't know the half of it," he replied and then he switched gears and asked me if I'd found something I'd want to wear? I showed him a couple of shirts along with a couple of pants that complimented the shirts. He gave me the nod of approval so we headed over towards the store clerk. The total came up to one hundred and twenty-two dollars. He acted as if he expected to pay more. I patted him on his shoulder and thanked him.

When we left Legends we stopped in Kohl's to get me a couple pairs of bra and panties sets. Bishop picked himself up a pair of dress socks and then we left the mall completely. On our way back to the hotel Bishop got yet another call. This time I could tell that it wasn't Katrina. He slowed his pace down so I could walk ahead of him. The tone of his voice changed too. It was no secret that he was talking to a woman. What she meant to him was a different question altogether. "I just left the mall," I heard him say. And then he laughed. "Trust me, you wouldn't want anything out of that mall. I only stopped in there to get a pair of dress socks for the funeral," he explained.

Telling the woman on the other end of the phone that she wouldn't want anything from Pembroke Mall only

UNIQUE

meant that she was a high maintenance chick. Judging from his conversation, I figured she only shopped at places like Barneys' or Saks'. And the fact that he reminded her about the choice of places she shopped meant that he remembered going on shopping sprees with her.

Meanwhile, during his intimate chat with a woman that was obviously his main squeeze, I noticed we were being followed by a black guy. He looked like an average cat, so it was hard to tell whether or not he was some random stalker or a hit man for Duke. I felt uneasy and right when I was about to get Bishop's attention, he suddenly disappeared. One minute he was in plain sight and the next minute he was gone. I started to back track my steps to see if he was lingering around one of the corners, but I changed my mind and continued to do what I came here to do in the first place.

Bishop was in his own world. His conversation with this woman lasted until we got in the lobby area of the hotel. When he realized his window for privacy was about to end, I heard him tell her he loved her too and then he ended the call. We got on the elevator and took it to our floor. As we exited the elevator I smiled at him and said, "It's good to know that some people are still in love."

He gave me this cute little look and said, "If you told me you loved me, I'd tell you the same."

"So, you're telling me that you tell people you love them even when you don't mean it?"

He stuck the key card into the door and opened it to let me inside the room. "What is that, a trick question?" he smiled.

CHEAPER *to* KEEP HER 2

I laid my things on the bed and took a seat next to them. "You know it's not a trick question. So, just answer it. All you've got to say is yes or no."

Bishop stood there in front of me and gave me the cutest smile ever. I was about to fucking melt. He was beginning to turn me on and the crazy part about all of this was that I knew he had someone in his life but I could really care less.

"Give me some time to think about it and then I'll get back with you," he said as he walked towards the bathroom. "Excuse me for a second. Gotta go to the men's room."

"Take your time," I replied.

After he stepped into the bathroom and closed the door I turned my focus to my things and began to sort them out. Meanwhile, I heard Bishop's cell phone ring from the bathroom. "Hello," I heard him say, and then he fell silent. A few seconds later he said, "I'm in room 512." And when he told the caller what room we were in, I knew right off the bat that it was Katrina he was talking to. Immediately after, he ended the call, he walked out of the bathroom and confirmed what I thought was true. "Katrina is on her way up to the room."

"Oh, really," I replied nonchalantly as I continued doing what I was doing.

By the time she knocked on the door, I was already in the bathroom trying to get out of my clothes so I could take a quick shower. I had no idea if they had plans for us to leave the room. But I figured if they did, I'd be ready.

"What are you doing here so early?" Bishop asked.

"We need to talk."

UNIQUE

"What's up?" I heard Bishop ask. I waited for Katrina to speak. I stood by the bathroom door quietly. I even found myself holding my breath. Unfortunately for me, all of what I did was done in vain because when I heard the hotel room door closed, I knew that they had taken their conversation into the hallway. I sucked my teeth and proceeded to take a shower.

While I bathed myself, I couldn't help but wonder what was so secretive that Katrina didn't want me to hear what she had to say to Bishop. Since I wasn't that close to Bishop, I knew it would be like pulling teeth to get him to fill me in on what she had to say. People are so shiesty these days that it wouldn't surprise me if that bitch was trying to plot on me. She'd better come correct because I'm not in the fucking mood. Especially with all the shit I'd been through with Duke's scandalous ass! I've vowed to stay two steps ahead of ever motherfucker I came in contact with. And that's my word.

I wasn't the bitch to fuck with anymore.

Scandalous Bitches

*I*t only took me about ten minutes to shower.

By the time I exited the bathroom Katrina and Bishop were back in the room. I looked at Katrina and said hello. She looked at me with a funny expression and acted as if she didn't want to speak back. I rolled my eyes. The shit didn't matter to me. But I did make it my business to put her stupid ass on Front Street. "You okay?" I asked.

"I'm fine," Katrina replied.

I immediately looked at Bishop. He shook his head while Katrina had her back turned. And then he said, "I am going to need you to stay here while Katrina and I head out to the club."

"How long are you going to be?" I asked.

"Not too long," he replied as he stuck the hotel key into his front pocket. Ten seconds later, he and Katrina were gone.

When the door closed I took a seat on the bed. There I was sitting in the room all by myself. I had no idea what I was going to do while they were gone. And that's when I realized I had no friends or family to call. I wasn't a bad person so why was I alone? At that very moment I thought back on my life and tried to remember how many people I had done wrong? I knew there were at least two men I had used for my own personal gain. But I didn't believe I caused this much karma. I mean, all I'd ever done was use those cats for their money. That was it.

So for me to go to jail for something I did not do was really fucked up. I can count the fingers on one hand for the times I did someone wrong. But I would need to use my hands and my feet to count the many times I had been done wrong. It seemed as if I couldn't get any sympathy from anyone around me. But when the shoe was on the other foot people were quick to point fingers. I couldn't express it enough about how it was going to be about me from this day forward. I was stepping on any and everybody's fucking feet to get where I got needed to go. No more Miss Nice Girl. I was going to be the biggest bitch ever. Fuck that! Nice Girl died in jail, now only the Bitch with Attitude was left.

Instead of being in the room I grabbed the key card and headed down to the lobby of the hotel. I figured getting some fresh air would take my mind off the bullshit I had running through my mind. I had no idea where I was going but I knew I needed to take a walk. I headed out to Virginia Beach Boulevard and headed toward Barnes and Noble bookstore. I didn't have a penny in my pocket to buy anything but I knew that I couldn't cause any harm by browsing through the books and magazines when I got there. Thank God the weather was nice, so my walk went fairly quick. I was greeted by one of the store clerks and was told that if I needed anything, don't hesitate to ask.

"Can you tell me where the African American section

is?" I asked.

The young lady pointed me in the right direction of the African American section was, I thanked her and went on my merry way.

When I was in jail I was turned on to a book called Keep the Faith by Faith Evans. My cellmate at the time was reading it and told me I had to read it. So I took it after she was done and when I read the first page I was hooked. So I figured since I'm not doing anything why not see if I can find another book by her. I mean who knows, I could probably read damn near an entire book while Bishop and Katrina were out.

While I glanced through the books in the urban section I noticed two men walking up behind me. They startled the hell out of me. I turned around and faced them both. One of them was a Caucasian male and the other one was Black. Both men were dressed in plainclothes but it wasn't hard to tell that they were detectives. I stood there with a puzzled expression because it had just dawned on me that this black guy was the exact same man who was following me earlier while Bishop and I was in the mall. I chuckled underneath my breath because now it came to me why he was following me. "You know I almost blew your cover earlier when I noticed you following in the mall," I stated.

"I'm glad you didn't," he replied as he extended his hand to introduce himself. "My name is Detective Whitfield and this is my partner, Detective Rosenberg. We're the investigators assigned to the murders and the illegal baby adoptions done by the hands of Duke Carrington."

I shook his hand and immediately let it go. I nodded

my head instead of saying a word. They were in my space, so I knew they had more to say than I did.

"Mind if we go somewhere more private?" Detective Whitfield asked me as he looked around at our surroundings.

"Sure, I don't mind. But where?"

"Let's go over there to that isolated corner," he suggested. I said okay and proceeded to walk in that direction.

I wondered if Whitfield was the one talking because both of us were Black or if he took the lead on all of their investigations. I hoped the latter. My radar was up, my trust level down. A gold badge and the same skin color as me weren't guaranteeing trust on my part.

Detective Whitfield and Rosenberg led me to the back of the bookstore. It was completely empty. There was no one in sight. There were only two chairs available so I sat in one of them while Detective Whitfield sat in the other, solidifying that he was the lead detective.

Detective Rosenberg stood next to his fellow detective as Whitfield prepared to make his spiel. Before he ran down certain details of their operation, he made it his fucking business to want to know who I was with at the mall? Before I gave up Bishop's name, I hesitated for a moment to gather my thoughts. Honestly, I hadn't known Bishop that long, so I really didn't have much to say about him. Not only that, that question alone made me feel awkward. I mean, I really wasn't comfortable talking about him . . . much less giving them his name.

So, while I contemplated what to say, Detective Whitfield interrupted my thoughts by saying, "Before you say anything, just know we'll be able to find out whether or not you're lying to us. And if we find out that you told us a lie then it's not going to look good for you."

I jumped on the defense. "What makes you think I'm gonna lie to you?" I blurted out.

"Listen Lynise, I just want everything to be laid out on the table so we can all be on the same page. That's it," he replied, trying to play it cool. He knew he had said the wrong thing to me, that's why he tried to soften the blow. I wasn't stupid and by the time this conversation of ours was over, he'd recognize it for sure.

Before I gave these clowns any information I rolled my eyes and chuckled underneath my breath. This whole scene with them surrounding me as if I was a fucking informant was pathetic if you asked me. I mean, you would think with all the technology and forensic investigators roaming these idiots would have all the information they need.

But no, they would rather be lazy and have non-compensated snitches do their work for them. Shit, if I was going to do their jobs for them, then they're gonna have to do more than give me immunity and a get out of jail free card. A bitch like me needed a roof over my head and a few dollars in my pocket. If they couldn't fit those amenities in their budget then I wouldn't be spilling my guts. They would get the bare minimal, if they got anything at all. And that was my word.

After Detective Whitfield changed his tone a bit, I finally told him what Bishop's first name was. He tried to get his last name out of me, but I swore to him that I didn't know it, which was the God's honest truth. I did however, tell them both that he was Neeko's older brother and that he was only here to bury him.

"Are you positive that he doesn't want to seek any revenge for his bother's death?" Whitfield wanted to know.

"If he does, he hasn't mentioned it to me," I lied. Again, these sorry ass detectives weren't trying to give up anything of value for the real scoop on Bishop, so I fed them enough to get them off my back.

"Did he mention when Neeko's funeral would be?" his questions continued.

"Not yet. But he and Neeko's girlfriend, Katrina, are making those arrangements as we speak."

"Well, you just make sure you keep your eyes and ears open. We want to know about every step they make. And if you hear anything about trying to seek revenge, please don't hesitate to contact us."

"I won't," I replied, even though I planned to do the exact opposite.

After Detective Whitfield grilled me for information about Bishop, he shifted his conversation to the plan they had to take Duke off the streets. I sat there and watched his body language as he gave me certain details about their operation. I also watched the other detective through my peripheral vision while he was watching me. These guys seemed to like they had it all figured out. But I wasn't sold on their elaborate plan to arrest Duke. It was bogus if you asked me. During those few months I had spent with Duke, I found out how vicious this guy really was. He didn't play games with anyone. He was notorious for eliminating anyone who'd gotten in his way. And if he didn't do it himself, he had people who'd jump at the opportunity.

Since the judge let me go, I had every intention on helping these detectives bring that bastard down. But I wasn't going to let them put my life in danger to accomplish their mission.

During the entire briefing, I believed I only had a handful of words to say. Detective Whitfield pretty much ran the floor. When our talk was finally over, he looked at me and asked me if I had any questions. I started to get up and walk away from his silly looking ass. But I stayed calm and said, "Do you really expect me to call him and ask him if he'd want to have dinner with me after all the shit I'd been through with him? I mean, that doesn't sound crazy to you? He's a very bright man and he's going to know that something isn't right."

"Detective Rosenberg already thought about that," Detective Whitfield retorted. "And all you have to do is play on the fact that even though he screwed you around and had you locked up for something you hadn't done, you still can't take your mind off of him."

I gave this guy the look of death. "Are you fucking kidding me? Is that all you have?" I spat. "Me telling that no good son of a bitch that I can't get my mind off him sounds suspect. He's not going to believe any of that bullshit. You're talking about a man who has pregnant women killed if they won't give their babies to him so he can sell them to his rich clients. He is heartless. There is no beating around the bush with this man. He will see right through that shit as soon as I open my mouth. If you can't come up with a better plan than that, then you're gonna have to find another chick to do your dirty work because I'm not about to get my fucking head chopped off because y'all ain't got y'all shit together."

Both detectives looked at me like I was crazy. "You need to calm down," Detective Whitfield said as he surveyed the bookstore to see if I had attracted any attention. "I know there's a better way that we can handle this."

"Not with that shit you're talking about!" I interjected. "I am not about to let y'all get me caught up in that mess and get my head blown off. Shit! I'm trying to live and maybe get married one day and have some damn kids." I abruptly stood to my feet.

Detective Whitfield grabbed me by my arm. "Where you think you're going?" he asked me.

"You better get your hands off of me," I roared. I was in a state of indifference. It was Whitfield's job to handle the black bitch in case I didn't go along with the program. Plus, no way did I want a white cop to touch me like this. Hell, I didn't want this muthafucka touching me like this.

Again Detective Whitfield surveyed the bookstore to see if I had caused people to look at us. He leaned in towards my right ear and said, "If you don't cooperate with us then I would personally make it so that you end up back in jail where you started. I don't have time for your games. The judge dropped the charges against you based on the condition that you help us. Now if you continue to give me problems, then I will make a call right now to the jail so they can start your paperwork while I transport your ass back down there."

"So now you're threatening me?" I snapped and then I snatched my arm away from him.

"I don't make threats. I make shit happen," he

snapped back.

Detective Rosenberg took one step toward us in effort to defuse the situation. I wasn't in the mood to hear a word he had to say. So I took the first step to leave. But before I could take the second step, Detective Rosenberg grabbed my arm as delicate as he possibly could. I stopped in my tracks and looked at his hand as it held onto my arm. And within three quick seconds I looked straight at him. "If you don't take your hands off me I am going to scream," I told him.

He immediately removed his hand from my arm. "Look," he began to say, "Look Lynise, my partner and I know you're bitter about this whole situation, but if you get on the same page with us, we can help you get the justice you deserve."

"Look, I understand everything you guys are saying, but I'm going to need to sleep on this tonight. So hand me your card and I will call you tomorrow."

Detective Rosenberg pulled a business card from his jacket pocket and handed it to me. I grabbed it from him and made my way out of the bookstore. I looked back a couple of times to see if I were being followed. And when I realize I hadn't, I dashed around the corner and power walked back to the hotel.

Wondering what in the fuck was I doing . . .

LET'S BE REAL

*W*hen I arrived back at the hotel I realized I
hadn't done anything I had set out to do.

I was right back where I started. And after I re-
entered the room, I slammed the door and sat back down
on the bed. I picked up the remote control and began to
surf through the channels. Unfortunately for me, there
wasn't a thing I wanted to watch on television. I started to
rent a movie from the demand channel but then I decided
against it because the room wasn't in my name. Bishop
probably would not have cared one way or another, but it
was the principal behind it all.

Since I had nothing else to do, I've decided to lie
down and catch a quick nap. With all the stuff I had
going on, I found it hard to close my eyes. So I just laid
there and stared up at the ceiling. The conversation I had
with the detectives kept replaying over and over in my
head. And the part that bothers me was the fact they
wanted to use me as fish bait to reel Duke's slimy ass in.
As bad as I wanted to see that bastard in jail, I wasn't
about to gamble with my life to do it. Not only that, I had
invested a lot of time and emotion fucking with Duke. I
needed compensation more than just simple gratification
and seeing him behind bars. I was broke and I had no

place to call home. I needed some type of funding. I needed a new wardrobe, a whip and a place to lay my head. So somebody was going to have to pay up or keep it moving. I was a chick from the streets and it was about time for everybody to know it.

I hadn't realized I had fallen asleep until the hotel door opened and closed. The way Bishop and Katrina walked in the room startled the hell out of me. She cut her eyes at me for a brief second and again she walked into the bathroom. Bishop on the other hand, took a seat in the chair by the table and asked me how long I had been asleep?

I looked over at the clock on the nightstand and said, "Not long. Maybe about forty-five minutes."

Bishop smiled. As much as I wanted to say it was a devious smile, I couldn't. It was just a simple smile. And for whatever reason, I didn't know how to take it.

I said, "Were you and Katrina able to handle your business?"

Bishop shook his head. "You will not believe what happened while we were out."

"What happened?" I whispered.

Before Bishop could utter another word to me, Katrina walked out of the bathroom. He and I both looked at her. Believe me, I felt a little awkward when she looked at me. To me, it was more of a stare than anything, which made me believe that she was probably eavesdropping on our little chat from the bathroom. I waited for her to come out of her mouth the wrong way because I wasn't going to hesitate to curse her stuck-up ass out.

"Have you decided what you are going to do?" Bishop asked.

Katrina took a few steps towards him while she was fixing her blouse. "I'm going to head back over the water. I figured while I'm over that side I could wait for that guy to call me."

"You sure you want to do that?" Bishop questioned her.

Without giving it much thought, Katrina said, "Yeah, I'm fine with it. I'll be all right. I mean, what can he do to me?"

"I just don't trust him."

Katrina turned towards the door and began to walk towards it. "Well, if I have any problems, then I'll give you a call."

Bishop sighed. "A'ight," he said and then he shook his head.

It didn't surprise me when that heifer walked out the door without saying goodbye. She's the type of chick who wanted everything her way and if she couldn't get it, then she'd make shit very difficult for everyone around her. When I worked at the club I always made it my business to avoid her. I did this to keep from fucking her up.

There were a few times when she got into a few arguments with a couple of dancers. Now I've got to admit that Katrina was one feisty bitch. But the two dancers she had the confrontations with were even crazier. Those chicks were from Portsmouth and they held their city down. So it would've been funny as hell to see them whip her ass. Thank God for Neeko. He was her savior 'round there. And she knew it too, which is why she kept running her fucking mouth. I wonder what she was going to do now. Neeko was dead and gone and he was no longer around to save her dumb ass?

"So where did you guys go?" I asked him.

Before he answered me, he placed his finger against his lips. "Shhhhh, let me see if she's gone," he said as he got up from his chair. He tiptoed over to the hotel door and gently turned the knob. When the door clicked, he pulled it open, trying to be as quiet as he possibly could and then he peeped out into the hallway. When he brought his head back into the room, he closed the door and said, "She's gone."

I laughed. "Don't tell me you're scared of her," I commented jokingly.

Bishop sat back down in his seat and said, "Come on now. Do I look like I'm scared?"

I cracked a smile. "I don't know now. You could be one of those guys that act all macho but as soon as a fight breaks out, you start running."

"Don't let the nice guy exterior fool you," he replied as he readjusted himself in the chair.

"So, are you going to tell me what happened?" I wondered aloud.

"Remember I told you how the books were adding up."

I nodded my head.

"Well, she tells me that she was instructed by Neeko to give some cat named Ty thirty grand to buy one and a half kilos of coke."

"Hold up now, that is a lie. For as long as I've known Neeko, I've never known him to deal in drugs."

"I said the same thing," Bishop commented. "So

when I told her I needed to see this guy, she came up with some lame ass excuse about how Neeko was the only one who had the guy's number, but she knew where most of these stash houses were.

"Did she take you?"

"Lynise, you won't believe the goose chase she put me on."

"Where did she take you?"

"She drove me around to every hood in the city of Norfolk."

"So I take it you didn't see him."

"No I didn't."

"So what are you going to do? Leave it alone."

"Hell no. I am not letting shit go! She is going to either show me who this nigga is so I can get my brother's dough back or let me take it out of her ass! Like I said before, I have never known Neeko to be involved in drugs. So in my opinion, she either has the money stashed away for herself and doesn't plan on letting anyone know about it. Or she has already spent it."

I could tell Bishop was getting a little aggravated because he was about to say something, but then he stopped. So to take the edge off and lighten up the mood, I smiled and said, "Don't get all bent out of shape. I know you've got a lot on your mind, but in the end everything is going to come together."

Bishop sighed heavily. Then he looked towards the ceiling, took a breath and looked as if he was going into deep thought. I wanted so badly to ask him what was he thinking about, but I decided against it. I mean, I was sure he thought I was cool, but he barely knew me. And when you barely know someone, it wouldn't be wise to tell them your most secretive thoughts.

A few minutes later, he told me to excuse him while he made a phone call out in the hallway. I acted as if I didn't mind at all. But knowing about everything going on with Neeko's murder, Katrina acting all weird and suspicious, and the fact I had a detective's phone number stored away in my pocket were enough for everyone involved in this shit to be on edge. I just hoped I come out on the winning end when it was time for the fat lady to sing.

SUICIDE MISSION

When Bishop walked back into the hotel room he told me to come with him.

I stood up from the bed and asked him where were we going? "I want you to take a ride with me," was all he said as he led me out of the room.

He refrained from talking to me while we waited for the valet to bring his vehicle around. Once inside, he couldn't keep his mouth closed. I sat there and listen to him vent about how he wished he would've come down here a lot sooner to help Neeko out with his business. He continued to harp on the fact of how Neeko used to always beg him to become his partner. And if he would've taken Neeko up on his offer, then he probably wouldn't have gotten murdered.

"Don't beat yourself up," I chimed in.

"You don't understand. Neeko was my baby brother. I was supposed to protect him and have his back in any situation. But look at him now . . . murdered. And the fucked up part about it is that I can't bring him back."

"Where are we going?" I attempted to change the subject. I figured the way this conversation was going, I'd hate to see Bishop go on a suicide mission, especially while I was with him. Hell, I was trying to live.

"Katrina just called me and told me to hurry up and get back across the water," he replied right after we got on Highway 264 from Independence Boulevard. He stayed in the far right lane as we headed towards downtown Norfolk. He had the gas pedal to the floor. I looked at the speedometer and I clearly saw that he was driving one hundred and ten miles per hour.

"You might wanna slow down a little because the state troopers around here stay on the alert for speed demons," I volunteered, but Bishop didn't take the heed.

"I can't think about them right now. I'm gotta get back to P-town and head up to the club before this person leaves."

Hearing Bishop just tell me that we were on our way to my old job in Portsmouth instantly gave me an anxiety attack. I tried to hold it back but I couldn't. My heart began to beat uncontrollably and I couldn't breathe. I reached for the power button to lower the passenger side window and then I literally stuck my head out of the window. Bishop looked over at me when I started exhaling and inhaling the outside air. "Are you okay?" he asked. I felt the speed of the truck slow down a little.

I wanted to explain to him what was going on with me but I couldn't open my mouth.

"Do I need to pull the truck over?" he asked.

I raised my hand and was finally able to open my mouth. "No, you don't have to pull over. I just needed some air," I told him.

"Are you sure?" he pressed the issue.

I brought my head back into the truck and sat straight up in the seat. I placed my hand across my chest and then

UNIQUE

I turned my attention towards Bishop. By this time, he had slowed his truck down just a little bit more, so I assumed we were driving at least eighty miles per hour.

"When you said you were going to the club, my mind couldn't wrap that thought around my heart. I mean, I haven't been back there since I was arrested. So I'm clearly not comfortable going there at all."

"What are you not comfortable with?"

"I worried about seeing Duke for one. And if I saw my ex-best friend named Diamond, then I'm gonna really freak out. Because I've wanted to kick her ass from the day I found out she set me up."

"Let me tell you something, you don't have to worry about Duke. You're with me and I'm not gonna let anything happen to you."

"What if it's beyond your control?" I interjected.

"Listen, just trust me," he said as he picked up more speed.

"I'm sorry Bishop, but my trusting gene has left the building," I responded. I mean, how could he come out of his mouth and tell me to do that? Didn't he get the fucking memo that I'd just gotten out of jail from trusting a nigga who cared two shits about me! Come on now, wake up! We live in a cruel fucking world. And to add insult to injury, he's only one person, so how in the hell will he be able to defend me against Duke and his wolf pack. I was sure Bishop had a gun of some sort in his possession, so I knew he felt confident to defend himself just in case he ran into an ambush. But poor little me would be a lost cause.

As he continued to drive towards the Portsmouth tunnel, my heart began to sink deeper and deeper into the pit of my stomach. Not knowing what was going to happen gave me an unsettling feeling. "Look Bishop, can you at least tell me why we're going over there?" I had to ask. I wasn't going to rest until I got that question off my shoulders.

"I just got off the phone with Katrina and she told me that there's this guy in the club who has some information for me concerning Duke and that cat who has Neeko's thirty grand."

"Well, that's good news. But don't you think she should've gotten that guy to meet you somewhere other than the club? I mean, I don't think it's a good idea to go up there."

"I understand your concern. But don't worry. I have everything under control."

After he gave me that explanation, I felt that there was nothing else to discuss. It was obvious I had reservations about going to the club. But since he felt differently, I realized I had to take this whole thing with a grain of salt. He said he'd take care of everything and that he'd make sure nothing happened to me, so I sat back in the seat and started praying to my Father in heaven. I knew he would be the only one that would be able to keep me out of harm's way.

Bishop took Portsmouth Boulevard's exit, crossed the railroad tracks and cruised around the C-shaped curve. The moment I laid eyes on the Magic City, I damn neared wanted to drop out of the passenger side of the truck. But when he told me to climb into the back seat of the truck while he was slowing down, I felt somewhat better. The windows of the Suburban were tinted really black, so it was entirely impossible for anyone going in or coming out of the club to see me.

"Do you see Katrina's car?" I asked him.

He scanned the parking lot immediately after he parked the truck. I searched the entire area myself and we didn't spot her vehicle. "Maybe she parked around back," I suggested.

"Maybe you're right. Let me go inside the club and see if she's in there," he said and then he got out of the driver's seat and assured me he'd be right back. I ducked down really low and peered over the passenger seat so I could get a full view of everything.

From where I was sitting, everything appeared to look the same. The parking lot was packed as usual with nice cars driven by niggas trying to either buy themselves some pussy or get themselves a hard-on from a lousy ass lap dance. Of course, I saw a few new faces strolling into the spot so they can make it rain. But the rest of the niggas I saw were the regular old scumbags that frequent the club.

I also saw a couple of fresh new faces that Magic City would soon swallow whole. These new chicks had absolutely no idea what they were about to walk into. I've seen dozens of strippers coming in on their high horse thinking they're gonna make grand money and meet a nigga who's gonna take them out of there, wife them up and put 'em up in a big ass house. But after about six months and none of the shit they thought would happen hasn't come to pass, then they start looking stupid and find themselves resorting to sucking dick and fucking their so-called knight in shining armor to get his attention and end up losing out.

I remember trying to school a couple of chicks when they started working for Neeko. They always started out being naïve and gullible. And after working their way around the club, they thought they were topnotch bitches! By then it was too late for those bitches because their heads were too stuck up in the clouds. And when it was all said and down, they were going to end up in the fucking gutter with their precious little dreams smashed. *Poor things!*

While I stay down in the back seat and scoped everything out, I noticed a fight about to break out. From what I could see, it appeared that two women were about to fight each other over this nigga. It seemed the girlfriend rolled up and caught her man talking to another chick. I couldn't hear exactly what they were saying. However, you could tell the main girl wasn't too happy to see her man sitting in the parking lot of a strip club talking to a stripper. The main girl friend had a little bit more weight on her then the stripper chick, so I would put my money down on the girlfriend if those two started brawling with one another.

Luckily for the stripper, the guy got out of his car and saved her from the ass whooping that was brewing up. While the guy tried to defuse the situation, I noticed a late model BMX X6 truck pulling into the parking lot. The way Bishop parked his truck between two other cars it wasn't possible for incoming vehicles to see it . . . or me. I can't explain the feeling that came over me when I rec-

UNIQUE

ognized that that X6 was the exact model and color Duke gave me to drive and then snatch it away from me the night he put me out of his place. It hurt just seeing my whip.

But that hurt wasn't nothing compared to the spear in the heart moment I had ten seconds later when his bitch, his so-called bride stepped out of my former whip. And to me, all of the shit occurred in slow motion. I was on the verge of snapping out was when the driver side door opened and Duke's bride stepped out of it. Within twenty seconds time, I had already played the shit over and over in my mind a dozen time. I damn neared lost my composure. My heart was telling me to run up on her ass and take my truck back. I mean, how dare that motherfucker take it from me and then give it to her. Hell, I took a lot of shit off him, so I deserved to behind the wheel of it. Not her.

While I battled with the thought of fucking her up and taking back what was rightfully mine, I couldn't help but notice how she strutted her stuck-up looking ass across the parking lot, with her Fendi bag draping her left shoulder. I couldn't see exactly what the bitch was wearing, but I saw the red soles underneath her heels. Christian Louboutin was written all over her feet. Not only that, I was shocked to see that she was more beautiful in person than she was in that newspaper photo. Jealousy and envy slowly crept into my heart as I sat up in the back seat and watched every step she took before she disappeared into the club.

Duke had really done it for me this time. He played with my heart, fucked me like I was some whore and then he threw me away to the wolves, so he could fuck the bitch I thought was my best friend. Then he slapped icing on the cake by marrying the most conceited bitch he could find. What a slap in the face. Normally niggas leave you for some gutter rat. But Duke changed the game on me and upgraded himself to the baddest bitch he could find in the Tidewater area.

A few seconds later, I looked down at the clock on the dashboard of Bishop's truck to get some idea of how long he'd been inside of the club. When I noticed that five minutes had went by, I knew it wouldn't be long before he'd be on his way back to the truck. But while he was in there, I wondered if he'd recognize Duke's wife if he got a chance to see her while she was inside. I wanted so badly to jump out of this truck so I could go inside to confront her. I felt as if she needed to see me so I could tell her all the fucked up shit her husband did to me. I wanted her to know the day I moved into the condo at the Cosmo building and the day I left. But I really wanted to tell her that I was the first chick pushing that BMW X6 she was driving, so in my mind she got the fucking leftovers. Something inside of me told me if he ever mentioned my name to her, it was probably to make himself look good. It wouldn't surprise me if she hadn't heard about me at all. But it was cool. I was gonna bounce back while his grimy ass was behind bars. And I was gonna have the last fucking laugh.

I looked back at the clock on the dashboard of Bishop's truck and realized that five more minutes had gone by. As I slowly lifted my head back up to turn my attention back towards the front door of Magic City, I was

UNIQUE

startled when I heard a loud explosion followed by a giant flash of light, then a fireball engulfed the entire club. Before I could process my thoughts, the fucking front door blew off the hinges, and the windows shattered into a million pieces, leaving shards of glass on the ground around the building. The left side of the club collapsed immediately after that.

Unbelievably, two of the strip club's patrons escaped from the front door. Neither man was recognizable because they were covered in debris. I jumped from the truck to see if one of them was Bishop. When I got within a couple feet of them, I knew that Bishop was still inside. My heart collapsed in the pit of my stomach and my mind had drawn a blank. I fought with the idea of running inside the club to see if I could find Bishop. But when I heard men and women screaming for help on the inside, I decided that it wouldn't be a good idea. I knew nothing about the proper way to rescue anyone from a burning building so I raced towards the other people in the parking lot hoping they'd already called the fire department and paramedics. When they informed me that they had, one guy that was standing out in the parking lot talking to a stripper said, "Oh shit! She's on fire!"

I immediately turned around and noticed that it was a stripper. She had on a long sleeve shirt and it was completely on fire. She screamed for help. The guy beside me took his shirt off and raced towards her. Seconds later, he threw his shirt over her back and wrestled her down to the ground. From that point, I witnessed her crying while the smoke from the flames escaped her body. I was in awe. I couldn't believe that I actually witnessed everything going on. But what really ate at me was that Bishop was still inside the club. And not even I could help him get out. I stood there speechless and I didn't know whether to wait around for the firefighters to get there or hop in his truck and leave.

A million things ran threw my mind. And the possibilities of Duke, his wife, Katrina and Bishop being burned alive gave me a bittersweet taste. I figured if he was in there with his new bride then they deserved to be in there. Although Katrina was a bitch at times, I didn't think she deserved this at all.

Bishop was on an entirely different level. I actually spent time with the brotha so knowing that he got caught up in that blaze put a damper on me. He was cool people. And he seemed like the type of cat who'd only fuck a person up if they messed with him. So to see this shit happen to him wasn't right at all.

Now that I think about it, it wouldn't surprise me if he got set up. I mean, out of thin air he gets a call saying he needed to get to the club. Come on now, something's not right with that. Then to see Duke's wife go inside the club right after Bishop seemed even sketchier.

While I tried to piece this whole scenario together, the firefighters finally arrived and asked everyone to move out of the parking lot and go to the other side of the street. I got back inside of Bishop's truck and move it to the opposite side of the street and decided to wait until I could find out who was all inside that club and if Bishop was dead.

My heart raced the entire time I sat there waiting to hear something. The thought of Bishop getting killed in that explosion became unbearable. And the one thing that kept nagging at me was the fact that Katrina had him come there. If she had never called him then he'd be at the hotel with me. It was too late to turn back the clock now.

THROWING SHIT IN THE GAME

*I*t took the firefighters two fucking hours to put out the flames.

The entire building was completely unrecognizable. It was damn near burned to the ground. I sat behind the wheel of the truck in disbelief and wondered when they were going to bring out the bodies.

People started coming out of the woodworks to see what was going on. A few family members stood by awaiting answers from the firefighters and hoping by some miracle that their loved ones were alive and well.

I recognized one woman who used to come into the club to borrow money from her daughter, who was a stripper. Her name was Ms. Dina and she was crying hysterically. All she kept saying was please don't let my daughter be in there. Her daughter's name was Kia, but her stripper name was Ecstasy. Ecstasy was one of the youngest dancers in the club and the prettiest one too. Her only downfall was that she let the niggas in the club feed her pennies. I used to tell her all the time that she was the prettiest chick with the baddest body out of all the other strippers in Magic City. If only she knew how to play her cards right, she'd be one paid bitch. I just hope she wasn't in the club so she could have another shot at life.

There were other people crying throughout the crowds. But I didn't recognize any of them. Meanwhile, as I took in everything around me, my heart nearly jumped through my fucking chest when I saw a silver 911 Porsche slowly cruising by the club. I couldn't see through the dark, tinted windows but there was no question in my mind that it was Duke behind the wheel of the car. I slid down in the front seat of Bishop's truck just in case the car stopped. I wasn't about to let him see me in no shape, form or fashion. So I quickly took precautionary measures.

I completely took my focus off the fact Magic City had just burned down with Bishop inside of it and watched Duke's Porsche as it combed the entire area. At one point I thought the car was going to stop, but it kept moving up the block.

I watched his car until it crossed over the railroad tracks and jumped on the Portsmouth Boulevard's ramp to get on the expressway. When his car disappeared around the loop that's when I exhaled. Seeing him ride by the club to check things out had just reconfirmed that he had eyes all over the place. If something happened in this city, Duke Carrington was definitely going to be informed about it. Now I knew that son-of-a-bitch was in complete control, which also meant he knew his wife was caught up in the explosion with everyone else.

So why the fuck didn't he stop?

His wife's car was right there in plain sight. There was no fucking doubt in my mind that he saw it. I mean, that move was really suspect if you asked me. This muthafucka really was that sinister and coldblooded. Whatever his reason was for not stopping would never be good enough to keep my mouth closed. The more fucked up shit Duke did, the more he made it painfully obvious that he cared about no one else but himself. I couldn't wait until the day I could see that man suffer.

And when it finally came, I was gonna spit on him after I put a bullet in the back of his fucking head.

It seemed as if time had been dragging along because an hour had gone by and not one body had been recovered yet. I had every intention to approach one of the firefighters but I knew it would be impossible to do. The police had the opposite side of the street blocked off with barricades and yellow tape. They had to make sure no one would be able to cross over into their crime scene.

I had to be honest and say that I had become very restless. The fact that more time had gone by and still not one body had been recovered made me realize that Bishop wasn't coming out alive. *So what in the hell was I going to do about it?*

I didn't have a cell phone in my possession, so I couldn't make one single phone call. I guess it didn't make any difference since I had no one to call. I did have keys to Bishop's truck, but he had the key card to the hotel room in his back pocket, so I had no idea how I was going to get back into the room. I swear I was always finding myself in a ton of shit. One day I was in jail and the next day, I was witnessing a strip club going up in

UNIQUE

smoke and killing almost everyone inside.

After three long hours had passed, several police officers asked everyone to clear the area. A few people started resisting. They knew they had lost their loved ones in the club fire. But everybody else left without giving the police any drama. I honestly didn't want to leave. I had Bishop's truck and it felt as if I was leaving him behind. Even though there was a great chance he hadn't survived the explosion, I still wanted to wait around to see them bring his body out of the debris and rubble. But since the police officers were adamant about clearing the area, I decided to come up with Plan B.

Tell me what's going to happen next?

My mind was racing and I was trying to stay cool. I presumed Bishop to be dead, while Katrina was missing in action and I was left in the dark with a lot of unanswered questions. As I drove away from the crowd, my mind went into overdrive. It wasn't a coincidence that both Bishop and Duke's wife walked into Magic City and five minutes later the whole fucking place blew up. And what's even more puzzling to me was the fact that Duke rode by to check out the damages without stopping. The last time I heard, he was supposed to be the new owner of Magic City. Seeing him do a drive by wasn't the type of behavior someone would do when it concerned his or her investment. They say what you do in the dark will come to the light. Whatever Duke had underneath his sleeve, he was going to reveal it in due time.

UNIQUE

I Need Some Answers

I hopped on the highway and headed back towards *Virginia Beach where I felt safe.*

This shit was surreal to me. If I had any fucking sense, I should have realized how crazy this whole thing was. I didn't need to be in the mix. Duke Carrington had cops and city officials behind him, and he was as slimy as they were. It was very hard to detect who was straight and who was crooked. Aren't those people paid to protect and serve?

During the course of the drive I rehearsed what I would say when I got back to the hotel. By the time I pulled up to the valet I was very confident the hotel clerk would give me a spare key card to get back into the room. When I walked inside the lobby I walked straight towards the desk clerk. Thankfully, the same night clerk was still on the clock because I didn't need any problems. All I wanted to do was get the spare key, carry my ass to the room and come up with a viable plan.

I cleared my throat while I looked directly at her na-metag and then I said, "Hi, Amy, do you remember me accompanying the guy from room 504?"

She smiled. "Yes, as a matter of fact I do," she replied.

I smiled back. "Good. I am so glad because I just dropped him off and forgot to get the room key from him. So I was wondering if you could either open the door for me or give me a spare, because I am exhausted and need to take a load off."

"I'm really not supposed to do that. But since I seen you two together a couple times then I'm gonna go ahead and make an exception."

"Thank you so much," I expressed. I was so damn happy she decided to give me an extra key. If she would've turned me down, then I would've been up Shit's Creek.

Immediately after she handed me the key I dashed towards the elevator. After I got on, I pressed the button for the fifth floor and waited for the elevator door to close. Moments after it closed, I felt a sense of relief throughout my entire body. The tension that had somewhat stiffened my neck had eased. This shit was crazy and madness and I was right smack in the middle of it all.

Right after I locked the door I sat down on the bed and used the remote to turn the television on. I went directly to Channel 10, which was my favorite local news station. When I realized the news had been on for at least seven minutes, I became agitated and fumbled with the remote control to turn up the volume. I couldn't tell if I missed the part about the explosion at the strip club, so I waited patiently and crossed my fingers, hoping that I hadn't.

After viewing the entire first and second segment, I

knew I had missed the footage from the club. Frustrated, I tossed the remote control on the other side of the bed and decided to take another ride. I wasn't going back to Portsmouth. I knew that wouldn't be a good idea. But driving over to Katrina's house would be. Finding out whether or not she was in the club at the time of the explosion became critical at this point. Something in my gut told me that things were really not what they seemed. One thing's for sure, my gut didn't lie to me.

When I walked back to the lobby, I passed the desk clerk again. She smiled and said, "You leaving again?"

I smiled back and told her that I needed to make another run. She advised me to be careful. I assured her that I would. After I got back in the truck and drove out of the parking lot, I noticed one of those standard types of police vehicles following me. It was dark out and the windows were tinted so I wasn't able to get a look inside of the car. For all I knew, it could be anybody behind the wheel. One part of me wanted to stop, get out of the truck, walk over to the car following me and demand the driver rolled down his window, so I could see who the fuck he was. The other part of me thought it was a bad idea. These people here in Virginia are crazy as a mother-fucker. I would be insane to try that stunt.

I hit the steering wheel with my fist and cursed the day that muthafucka driving the other car was born. *I mean, what was it with me? Why the fuck everybody and their damn mama wanted to fuck with me?* For as long as I can remember I'd never done anything malicious to anyone. I was known for giving people my last. If I had it and you wanted it, then it was yours. Point blank and end of story.

Two miles into the drive, I decided to get some distance between me and that asshole following me until I found an escape route. I pressed down on the accelerator harder and found myself with at least eight cars between us. My adrenaline pumped inside me like fuel. The further I gained distance on them the better off I felt. "Yeah, you bastard! You can't fuck with me! I'm a beast!" I screamed out loud, even though I knew no one else could hear me. It felt good though.

I noticed I was coming up towards Rosemont Road, which would be a perfect escape route to dodge the car following me. Has started to cross through the service station on the corner but there was too much light and the parking lot was filled with patrons, so I elected to make a sharp right turn at the street light and then I shot through the traffic light on Bonney Road. I then jumped on the ramp to head back towards Independence Boulevard. When I looked in the rearview mirror I saw a few cars behind me, but none of the cars was the one following me.

I let out a sigh of relief but I dared to slow down. The nigga I was fucking crossed me. My best friend betrayed me. The one man I believed was on my side had just been lured into a death trap. So once again I was all alone. And not having any of the answers I was looking for made my journey a little bit harder to travel. Although I lost the car following me, it still bothered me that I didn't know who in the fuck was tailing me. Not only that the thought that the car found its way back to the hotel and awaited my arrival made me feel uneasy. I figured the only way to avoid that from happening was that I couldn't go back. But then I figured, if I chose not to return to the hotel, then where would I go? I had so many questions but not enough answers which made me sick to my stomach.

Hell, it was a standard type of police vehicle but I didn't know if it was the cops in a so-called unmarked car or one of Duke's goons. I kinda laugh when I thought about the cops and unmarked cars. Every damn body in the 'hood knew when one of their whips came around. Regardless of how old, or new, the cops never fooled anyone with their so-called unmarked cars.

After driving for approximately five minutes, I got off the Military Highway exit, made a U-turn, got back on Interstate-264 and headed back in the direction of Katrina's house. Since there was no traffic, I arrived in her neighborhood in less than nine minutes flat. It seemed as if the closer I came to her house, the harder the flutter in the pit of my stomach jumped around.

I held on to the steering wheel with my left hand and rubbed my stomach with my right. It seemed like every time I got myself mixed up with unnecessary drama, my body always found a way to shut down on me. As much as I wanted to turn around and leave this situation alone, I thought about those young women who had been victimized by Duke and his flunkies, and I knew it wasn't just about me, it was about them. So that alone gave me the courage to move forward and take Duke down by any means necessary.

I noticed Katrina's house from a block away sitting in the cul-de-sac between two larger homes. I had to admit that the house was beautiful, but I didn't believe she deserved to live in it. I knew Neeko for years so I knew the blood, sweat and tears he put into buying this house. It was no secret he was a hard ass but everyone also knew he was no-nonsense when it came to his money. I remembered him telling me one day that he'd never get married, because he didn't want to get a divorce and a wife walking away with everything he worked so hard for. And now that I thought about it, I didn't blame him.

I drove slowly towards the house and noticed all the lights were turned off, but Katrina's car was parked in the driveway. Seeing this puzzled me. A couple of hours ago she called Bishop and told him to meet her at the club. From the way Bishop explained it to me, Katrina was already inside the club, which was why he and I suggested that her car would be parked around back. Now if all of this was true, her car shouldn't be parked in her driveway. It should be buried underneath the debris from the fire and explosion from the club.

Now here I was posted up outside the house my former boss owned, wondering whether or not I should call Detective Whitfield and tell him what I knew. I mean, it wouldn't hurt. And besides, what else was I going to do with this information? I had no one else to call. Even if I did, the last time I put myself in that type of predicament, I was railroaded. Yes, bamboozled.

If Diamond never taught me anything in life, she taught me that I should never trust anyone. Not even your best friend. I still couldn't get over Diamond's betrayal. I had known this bitch almost all my life and the thing I took away from the relationship was there was no such thing as loyalty. I was sure when she went to Duke and

UNIQUE

schooled him about my blackmailing scheme, he promised her the world on a silver platter. Additionally, I knew he even threw a few dollars at her so she could keep her fucking mouth closed. I swear, life had definitely taught me some valuable lessons. Too bad I had to learn the hard way.

Shit, I hoped I didn't have any more lessons to learn.

When I saw all I needed to see, I turned Bishop's SUV around and headed back in the direction I came. I hurried up and got out of the neighborhood before I was spotted by Katrina or one of her accomplices. It only took me about three minutes to jump on the nearest ramp to the expressway, which was good considering the distance from Katrina's house. Once I felt I was in the clear, something on the inside of me convinced me to ride by the old apartment I used to share with Diamond. I had no plans to stop. I just wanted to see if I saw any type of movement from outside, since I couldn't say for sure that she had gotten caught in the fire. I wanted to ask the other stripper who'd gotten a chance to escape the fire, if Diamond was in there. But she had gotten burned so badly that she wasn't in any shape to talk at all.

Now I knew this was horrible to say but if Diamond had died in that fire, I figured it was good for her. For the past couple of years, she had one foot in the club and the other one in the grave. It was only a matter of time before she would meet her maker anyway. I remembered saving her from getting her head blown off twice. One time she was caught trying to steal money from this nigga while she was sucking his dick back in the champagne room. When he realized what she was trying to do, he damn neared beat her to death with his pistol. I was furious when I found out what had happened. The only thing I could do for her was take her to the emergency room to get treated. The doctor and nurse who saw her wanted to know who beat her like that, and all she did was lie to them. I was stunned. But hey, what could I do?

The other time I saved her dumbass was when her ex-boyfriend fucked her up after he found out she was fucking with another nigga behind his back. Their altercation lasted for at least thirty minutes. When the police finally got to our apartment, that nigga had gotten away. Diamond's silly ass laid there on the floor, crying her poor little heart out, saying how tired she was with her life and that she didn't want to live anymore. Quiet as it was kept, that bitch played like she wanted to commit suicide. But I knew damn well she wasn't about to kill herself. She was a drama queen to the tenth power. And all she wanted was somebody to feel sorry for her because of all the fucked up decisions she made in her life.

I listened to her bullshit from time to time. But when I was tired, I tuned her ass out and focused on more important things. All and all, Diamond was a basket case. She was also a hoe with a lot of bark and no bite. So, if her body was found underneath all the rumble inside Magic City, then she finally got what she deserved.

A part of me still wish I was the one to put her monkey ass under.

UNIQUE

Sneaking Around Town

*D*iamond and I shared an apartment in the 'hood. The apartment complex wasn't low-income housing or Section Eight property, but it wasn't far from it. As usual a couple of the streetlights were blown out, so certain parts of the complex were left in the dark. Under normal circumstances I wouldn't be out here by myself. This apartment complex had a reputation for a lot of burglaries, old ladies getting their purses snatched and guys selling dope from at least one apartment in each building. But tonight I had to do things differently. I figured if I stayed in the truck with the doors locked I'd be okay. So that's exactly what I did.

I parked the SUV in the parking lot directly across the street from Diamond's apartment. I backed the truck into a parking space so I could see everything in front of me. For the first fifteen minutes I watched at least one hundred cars coming in and out of the complex. You didn't have to be a rocket scientist to see that something illegal was going on. If I were a cop, I would be knee deep in paperwork after arresting all of these hustling ass niggas.

And what was so crazy about it was that none of these guys tried to hide it. They literally held the drugs in their hands in plain view and did hand-to-hand transactions. They were off the chain. As much as I wanted to call them complacent, I couldn't. They knew the only way a cop was coming this way was if some fool had been shot and killed.

When I wasn't counting the transactions those niggas were making, I periodically glanced over at Diamond's bedroom window to see if there was any movement. Like Katrina's house, all of Diamond's lights were turned off. So there was no question in my mind that she wasn't home. After sitting there for over an hour I grew tired and decided to carry my ass back to the hotel. The key to the truck was already in the ignition. When I started the engine this guy came out of nowhere and startled the hell out of me. He approached the truck from the driver side door and tapped on the window lightly. I damn near jumped out of my skin. "Yo' shorty, you need something?" he asked.

When I turned my head completely around in his direction, I instantly recognized him. I let out a sigh of relief and then I pressed down on the control button to roll down the window. He smiled once he realized who I was. "What's up sis? Whatcha' doing out here? I thought you was locked up?" he said.

"Who told you I was locked up?" I asked him. I wanted to know what he knew about me before I volunteered any information. You see, T.J. was this seventeen-year-old, small time weed pusher from the neighborhood who hung out all times of the night, so he basically knew something about everything that happened around here. He lived with his aunt and she had an apartment in the next building over from Diamond's place.

"I was out here the night the police took you to jail. But everybody around here was talking about how you got a couple of bodies and that you wasn't gon' ever see daylight again."

"Well, whoever told you that don't know what the hell they talking about. I caught another charge and when they couldn't prove that I did it, they had to let me go."

T.J. looked at me in a suspicious manner. "You sure you ain't working for the police? A lot of bitches and niggas are doing it these days."

"For your information, I am not one of those bitches. I got locked up for some shit I didn't even do. So the judge had no other alternative but to let me go."

"So what are you doing around here? Why are you parked across the street from where you used to live at? Whatcha doing squatting on that stripper bitch you used to live with?"

I have to admit, TJ caught me off guard with that question. And even though I'm sure he wasn't the smartest kid in school, he had plenty of street sense. So I am sure he would smell my lie before I'd uttered one word. I knew I wouldn't be able to tell him what I was really doing, but at the same token, I had to tell him something that would seem plausible. Without blinking an eye I came up with a good explanation about why I was posted up in someone else's truck, watching Diamond's apartment from across the street.

First, I told him Diamond owed me some money and

that every time I called her she wouldn't answer her phone. I even lied and told him that I had been by here a few times and she wouldn't open the door, because she knew what type of car I was driving. So I finished off my lie and told him that the only way I will be able to catch her was by staking her apartment out in someone else's vehicle. After I laid out my fabricated story he gave me a nod of approval and cracked a smile.

"If it's like that, then I can't fault you," he said. "It's gotten so bad out here that niggas would do just about anything to get out of paying you your dough. Shit, I wish a nigga would try to buck on me and not pay me my paper. It would look like fireworks out here after I spit out all these lead pellets in this muthafucking burner." T.J. lifted his shirt to show me his gun as he talked his shit.

I burst into laughter. "You better put your shirt down boy before you fuck around and hurt yourself," I told him.

"Oh, trust me, I know how to handle this pistol. Ask any of these niggas 'round here. They'll tell you how I would blast a nigga in his ass real quick."

"Look, T.J., you need to calm your ass down."

"I'm calm."

"Well, if you call that calm, then I would hate to see you when you get pissed off."

While T.J. and I went back and forth about how mucho he was, his attention drifted away from me, so I followed his eyes. Before I could zoom in on the moving target, he said, "There goes your girl right there."

My heart dropped. Seeing Duke's silver Porsche pull

up outside of Diamond's apartment felt somewhat surreal. I had just gotten the answer I had been waiting for all night. Diamond was not inside of Magic City when it went up in smoke. *But why not?* Her shift always started at seven o'clock in the evening.

I knew one thing, this whole thing was becoming scarier and more sinister by the minute. Shit, it was starting to have a physical effect on me. My legs felt like they were about to become numb from dealing with this shit. And as I watched Diamond get her trifling ass out the passenger side of Duke's Porsche, it felt as if I had an anxiety attack coming on. I took a couple of deep breaths and then I exhaled.

One of the things fucking with me was this muthafucka's wife had just died in the fire and explosion that he probably was behind, and instead of playing the role of the grieving husband, he was hanging around with this worthless bitch. I didn't know whether to admire the set of balls on Duke, or be appalled. Regardless, I still wanted his bitch ass dead and six feet under.

"That nigga gotta be selling drugs because you can't cop a whip like that with a regular job." T.J. commented as we both witnessed Diamond close the passenger side door of Duke's car. "Every time that nigga pick her up or drop her off niggas around here be gritting on him. He don't ever get out of the car when he come out here, so don't nobody knows how he look. That nigga, Craig, from building four said if he ever catch homeboy outside his whip, he gon' rob his ass and take his car for a joy ride."

"How often does he come out here?" I wanted to

know.

"He comes out here almost every day. If he ain't picking her up, he's dropping her off."

"Did you see him pick her up today?" I continued to question T.J. If he tells me that Duke did in fact pick her up today, then she had to be in the car with him when he rode by the club tonight.

"Nah, I been out here all day and this is my first time seeing that car today," he replied.

Instead of drilling T.J. with more questions, I turned off the ignition and stepped out of the truck. When I planted both of my feet on the ground I immediately became nervous. T.J. looked at me like I was crazy. "Whatcha getting ready to step to her?" he asked.

The fact that T.J. had reminded me about what I was about to do, made me want to stop and think of another way to approach this situation. Don't get me wrong, Diamond wasn't your typical Laila Ali. She wouldn't step on a sour grape in a fruit fight. She was one of those bitches that would talk shit to you but when you step to her she'd back down every single time. So I wasn't worried about her throwing her fists up. I was more worried that she'd call him and tell Duke where I was. I was sure with his connections he knew I was out of jail. His ass had everyone from bail bondsmen, prosecutors and city councilmen on his payroll. But what he didn't know was where I was.

T.J. chuckled. "Don't beat her ass too bad," he said. I looked back at him with uncertainty, even though I knew she was no match for me. I tried to come up with a quick plan on how I would approach her. She had about two hundred feet from the parking lot to her apartment. If I wanted to get to her before she had time to get into her apartment and close the door, then I needed to sprint across the street right now. But when I tried to lift one foot up from the ground, it seemed impossible. I don't know if I was in shock or what. But I knew that something wasn't quite right with me.

"Why you just standing there? I thought you wanted to run up on her, so you can get your dough?"

I wanted to answer T.J. but my heart was beating louder than I thought.

"You better get over there before she get to her apartment," he warned me. It was like TJ was coaching me into doing something I knew wouldn't have a good outcome. With all the feelings I had harboring in my heart for Diamond, I knew if I came within two feet of her, I would seriously do some damage to her. Who knows, I'd probably catch a murder charge when it was all said and done. And then I will be right back in jail and I wouldn't be getting out.

"Screw her. She ain't worth it. I'll catch up with her grimy ass later," I finally said and then I realized I was able to move my feet again. I chuckled to myself. "God has a funny way of working things out," I uttered quietly.

"Whatcha say?" T.J. blurted out.

"I'm talking to myself," I told him and then I turned around and got back into the truck.

When I started the truck up and revved the engine, T.J. leaned towards the driver side window and said, "Want me to shout her ass out whenever I see her coming outside again and tell her that you were looking for?"

"No. Don't tell that bitch shit!"

"Good. 'Cause I really don't like the bitch anyway. She got smart with me a couple of months ago and she think I forgot all about it."

"That's just how she is. She doesn't fuck with anyone who she can't benefit from. But trust me, her fucking days are numbered. I just wish I would've known you didn't fuck with her like that, because I wouldve gotten you and one of your homeboys to run up in her spot to get all my shit I left in there before I got bagged up by the police. That is, if the bitch hasn't gotten rid of it herself."

"Boy, I would've loved to break into her shit. Me and my boys haven't done that shit in a long time. So it would have been funny as hell," T.J. expressed as he smiled.

I let out a long sigh. "Glad to know. So I guess I'll hit you up later. As a matter of fact, give me a number."

"You got something to write with?" HE asked me.

"Wait, hold up," I told him as I searched in the armrest of the truck for an ink pen. When I found one I also grabbed a business card Bishop must've taken from someone prior to him coming to Virginia. The business card was from a chick by the name of Karen Wheeler, who happened to be a mortgage broker from Newark, New Jersey. From the looks of her photograph, she was a very attractive woman. Too bad she wouldn't be talking to him anymore.

Immediately after I scanned the front of the business card, I flipped it over and began to write down T.J.'s cell phone number. After I was done I assured him that I would be giving him a call.

"Take care of your business Ma."

UNIQUE

"I will."

T.J. walked away from the truck and then I slowly exited the parking lot. Before I drove away, I noticed she turned on the light in the living room and then three seconds later the bedroom light came on. I shook my head because I realized that nothing about her had changed. Not even her movement throughout her apartment. Like clockwork, she'd always turn on the living room light as soon as she walked into the apartment, followed by her going straight to her bedroom and turning on the light as well. She was afraid of the dark. She would never sleep without some kind of light around her. Her TV ran all night long most of the time. I've heard people say that when a person is afraid of the dark, that's because they are the devil. I never believed it until now.

It was only a matter of time before the fires of hell rain down on her stupid, scary ass.

WHERE THE FUCK AM I GOING NOW?

I wished like hell I could've gotten a chance to beat Diamond's snitching ass up.
Luckily for her, I changed my mind and decided to come at her another way. I realized I do a lot of things on impulse. I never really thought things out, which was why things around me always seemed to fall apart.

As I drove away from the old neighborhood it dawned on me that I had nowhere to go. I couldn't go back to the hotel for fear that my life could be in danger. So where in the hell was I going to lay my head tonight? One part of me wanted to stick my pride in my pocket and call my ex-boyfriend Devin. Sure he was a self-centered asshole who couldn't keep his dick in his pants. Besides the issues with his cheating he was a big liar. I couldn't count the times that sorry ass nigga got caught in a whole bunch of lies. After a couple of years of his bullshit I finally threw in the towel. Don't get me wrong, Devin was a handsome ass guy. He even had a body to die for, and did I mention how good his fuck game was? He had my dumb ass open. I couldn't see the forest from the trees. Anything he said was always written in stone. Self-esteem issues were a huge factor in that relationship.

So today, I was so glad I could call him tonight and ask him to let me sleep over and not feel the pressures of fucking him to do so. After all, the bastard owed me. And I intended to collect. I mean, all I wanted was a warm bed to sleep in tonight and in the morning I would be gone.

I wasn't sure if he had the same number but nothing beats a failure but a try. I pulled over to a service station off Military Highway, because I noticed they had a pay phone outside. Bishop had a lot of change in the armrest, so I dug in and grabbed two quarters. It felt foreign for me to be using a pay phone. I mean, who done that these days? Everyone I've run into had a cell phone, so I couldn't believe that pay phones still existed. Not to mention, who'd think I would need to use one? I felt really weird.

After I dialed Devin's cell phone number I crossed my fingers and hoped that he'd answer my call even though he didn't recognize the number. He was big on not taking calls when he didn't recognize the number. I just hoped that this time it would be different. The phone rang four times on my end and when it sounded as if it was about to go to his voicemail, I hurried up and disconnected the line. When the money fell down into the change tray, I retrieved it and pushed it back into the change slot and began to dial his number again.

"Devin, answer this time," I said to myself. To no avail, he didn't pick up the second time. I am a firm believer that things happen for a reason, which only meant that it wasn't meant for me to get in touch with him. Instead of calling him again, I hung up the phone again and got my ass back into the truck.

I sat there for a moment and tried to figure out what I was going to do next. I thought about sleeping in the backseat of the truck. But either God or my gut told me to go back to Katrina's house. I knew this sounded really insane on my part but I figured if I played on that bitch's intelligence and acted like a distraught chicken with my head cut off, then she may have a little bit of sympathy for me. Trust me, I knew how to play the victim role. I even knew how to act like a dumb blonde. Then hoes like Katrina would think that you're naïve and would feel secure around you. My motive right now was to get in good with this chick without making her feel suspicious. At the end of the day, I needed to get out of the streets and even though I had reservations, I had to help the cops out. And if it took getting close to this cutthroat bitch, then so be it.

Thinking about the horrible death of Bishop began to weigh heavily on my mind. I knew I had only known him for less than twenty-four hours, but he made an impact on me in those hours I spent with him. For the first time in my life, I shared time with a man who had someone else's best interest in heart besides his own. I had ran into a lot of selfish men in my day, so I couldn't express enough about how sorry I was that he got caught up in all of this mayhem going on in this town behind Duke Carrington.

The thought that Bishop could've asked me to walk in the club with him gave me the chills. I mean, if he had I

UNIQUE

would be dead right now. And the sad part about it was, no one would've cared. I raced back to Katrina's house believing that Duke wouldn't be there because he'd just dropped Diamond off at her apartment. And even if he hadn't dropped Diamond off it would seem too risky for him to hang out at Katrina's house anyway. Since the club exploded, and people died, an investigation had to be underway soon and all parties would be scoped out, if not investigated altogether.

Finally, when I pulled up to her house I noticed another car in the driveway and there were a few lights on in the house. I was somewhat hesitant to proceed to her house because of the other car being there. After I realized the 2010 Audi belonged to Neeko, I let out a sigh of relief.

I parked Bishop's SUV alongside the curve in front of the house. Katrina must've heard the engine from the truck because right before I turned it off and pulled the key from the ignition, she peeked through the blinds in her bedroom window. I was sure I scared her by pulling up in this truck, so to put her at ease I got out so she could see that was I was alone. I couldn't say how she was feeling, nor could I tell you what was going through her mind, but I do know she wasn't prepared for what I was about to throw her way. I put on an expression of pure exhaustion. I knew I had to be dramatic so I rushed up to the front door and rung the doorbell frantically. It took Katrina longer to get to the door than I expected. Generally, when someone is ringing your doorbell or banging on your door hysterically, then you'd be in a rush to find out what was causing this person to act like that.

Not Katrina though. Whatever she was doing that prolonged her from answering the door was obviously more important. I just hoped that she wasn't making a phone call to Duke. If she were, then I knew I wouldn't leave here alive tonight.

Before she answered the door I said a quick prayer. I knew only God would be able to protect me from all of this mess that was going on.

"What's the matter, are you all right?" she asked immediately after she let me into her house.

I tried to produce some fake tears but I couldn't. So I became a little more dramatic and said, "Katrina, Bishop is dead."

Katrina acted like she was surprised. Right then and there I knew that this bitch was a heartless ass snake. It appeared to me that she didn't think Bishop told me he was meeting her at the fucking club. So I played the dumb role just to see where she wanted to take it.

After she close the front door she led me into her kitchen and had me sit down in one of the kitchen chairs. "Katrina," I uttered, "Bishop asked me to take a ride with him to the club so he can meet someone. And as soon as he went inside the whole place went up in flames."

"What? I am not understanding you," Katrina replied, sounding confused as she stood up next to me. She placed her hand over her heart and said, "You're saying Magic City went up in flames?"

"Yes. That's what I am saying. And it didn't blow up until Bishop and some other lady went inside."

"How do you know Bishop went inside?" she probed me for answers.

UNIQUE

"Because I watched him from the truck," I told her.

"Oh my God!" she said and started pacing around in the kitchen. "This can't be. My heart can't keep taking all of this. First, it was Neeko. And now it's Bishop and the club."

"What are we going to do?" I asked her. I wanted to get in her head and get as much information out of her as I possibly could. I figured as long as I played silly, then she'd give up the goods.

"I don't know," Katrina replied as she continued to pace the kitchen floor. I watched her body movement closely. If Bishop hadn't hipped me to what was going on and how sneaky she had become, then I would be clueless as hell. She could've pulled the wool over my eyes and I would not have noticed.

"We got to do something," I added. "We gotta call the police and tell them that Bishop was one of the people who died in the fire. And that Duke was behind all of it."

"No. No. No. That wouldn't be a good idea," Katrina replied. Her whole facial expression changed. She acted as if just the mention of the name Duke spooked her.

"Well then, what are we going to do? We can't just sit here and act like it didn't happen," I protested. I wanted to test her out and see what I needed to do to press her buttons.

"You got to give me a minute to take all of this in. Right now, I can't think straight. I mean, I need to sit down and collect my thoughts." She took a seat in the chair next to me. I watched her bury her face in her hands. She stayed in that position for about ninety seconds. And when she lifted her head she seemed as if she was in a fucking daze. And for the first time, she looked like she was really sad by this whole ordeal. Tears were literally falling from her eyes. I swear I couldn't detect whether this bitch was faking or not.

I reached over and rubbed her shoulder. I had to pretend that I cared. "It's going to be all right," I told her. Truthfully, I didn't even know if I believed that shit. Hell, I didn't know what was what at that moment. Was this bitch that good of an actress or was she genuine and really felt bad that first Neeko, and now Bishop was possibly dead.

She shook her head at me. "Lynise you just don't understand."

"I do understand," I tried to assure her as I continued to rub her shoulder.

She snatched away from me abruptly and jumped up from the chair. She scared the shit out of me. "No you don't!" she snapped.

At that moment, I knew she had come to the end of her rope and she was holding on for dear life. She looked like a woman running from an abusive husband. And I could tell that she wanted to confide in me, but was hesitant because she didn't know if she could trust me or not.

If you want to know the truth, she was the bitch that couldn't be trusted.

When you run into a person who has problems with trusting others it's because they've been hurt or they've fucked up every relationship they had. To be around them is toxic. And they'd suck the fucking life out of you if you let them. Now the problem with this situation was I didn't know Katrina well enough to decide which type

UNIQUE

person she was. So I figured the best way to handle her was play this whole thing by ear, which meant to listen more and say less. At least until the real snake showed yourself. *Was she a cobra waiting to put me to death? Or a garden snake, harmless as they came?* But to put that remedy into effect I knew I had to open the door.

"Look, Katrina, I know that you and I really don't know each other. But the fact we share a common bond through Neeko should account for something. Now Neeko wasn't the nicest person in the world and we hardly ever saw eye-to-eye. But when I was hauled off to jail for a crime I didn't commit, he was the only person that came down there to see me. He was the only person who offered to help me. So if I don't do anything else, I will do what I can to make Duke pay for his murder since his brother, Bishop, isn't here to do it for him."

After I expressed my feelings to Katrina she stood in front of me with a blank expression. I couldn't tell whether she was going to break or not. So I waited.

Finally, after standing there for almost one long minute Katrina wiped away her tears with the back of her hands and then she sat back down in the seat next to me. "Lynise, I know you want to help put Duke in prison for a long time. But when I tell you that this thing is bigger than Duke, believe me."

"What do you mean?" I asked. I needed some clarity because she was starting to scare me.

Katrina hesitated for a moment and then she said, "I've known Duke for a very long time. In fact, I cheated with him during a brief break up Neeko and I had. No one else knows this but my second child is Duke's."

I caught a lump in my throat. "Are you serious?" I asked in mere shock. I never thought in a million years that she would be telling this. My heart started racing sixty-five miles per hour while I waited for her to pour the rest of her heart out to me.

"For years I walked around with all this guilt buried in my heart, and everyday when I had quiet moments with Neeko, I wanted so badly to tell him." She paused and I knew she was trying to maintain her composure. "But I couldn't get up the nerve to do it. Not only would it have affected him, it would've affected my youngest daughter as well. And I didn't want to ruin the bond that those two had."

"Does Duke know that your baby girl is his?" I interjected. I couldn't hold it back. That question was killing me.

"Yes. He knows. And that's why he's been able to handle me the way he has."

"What do you mean he handles you?"

Tear after tear started falling from her eyes once again. She couldn't control them with her hands. "You've heard about all that real estate and other investments Duke has right?"

I nodded.

"Well, he didn't get all of that on his own. He borrowed over ten million dollars from some very wealthy men who happen to be some no-nonsense powerful brothers. And when they gave Duke that money, he agreed to have their money along with interest back in their hands in a certain amount of time. But guess what? It didn't happen. So guess what they did?"

"What?"

"They roughed him up and then they torched Duke's mother's house while she was out running errands. But they told him that if he didn't come up with at least a third of the money they lent him soon, then they were going to make sure that when they torched her new place she would be in it."

"Get the fuck out of here!" I commented. Hearing all of these details about those two dangerous men made me feel like I was biting on more than I could chew. And that's when I realized that she was right. Every single thing that was happening around us was definitely much bigger than Duke.

"Lynise, you and me aren't going to be able to touch Duke," Katrina said matter-of-factly. "The police can't even touch him."

I shook my head. "No, I don't believe that," I told her.

"Well, believe it, because it's true. I mean, how do you think he was able to run an illegal adoption ring without getting busted? The police knew that Duke had that doctor take a lot of those babies without their mothers consent. And they knew that Duke was responsible for those young girls who got murdered a few hours before they gave birth."

"So what are you telling me?" I asked, even though I already knew the answer.

"I'm telling you that we're gonna have to walk away from this and act like it never happened."

"Why? Because he has those police on the payroll?" I snapped.

"No. None of those policemen work for Duke. They work for those two brothers."

"Wait, now I'm confused."

"Listen Lynise, and listen carefully. The policemen around here are like watch dogs for those men. They are paid to look after Duke until they get all their money back. So in other words, Duke is like their property and they aren't going to let anyone fuck with him. And I do mean no one. Not even Bishop could've gotten close to Duke."

"How did Duke know that Bishop was in town?"

"The day after the police found Neeko's body, Bishop got word and drove down here in a matter of hours. And as soon as he got here, he went straight to the club and started asking questions. So, when Duke found out he was here, he called me and told me to hand him over or else."

"Well, if you knew that it was that hot around the club then why didn't you tell Bishop?" I asked. I figured since she opened up to me about all the skeletons that were hidden in Duke's closet, then it would be easy for her to explain to me why she led Neeko's brother to believe that he could vindicate his death.

Continuously wiping tears away, Katrina took a deep breath and said, "Bishop and I never saw eye-to-eye from day one. He told Neeko that I was a gold digger and that he shouldn't trust me. So, after I heard all of that, I started disliking Bishop, too. And besides, I was in control of Neeko's books, so when Bishop started asking a lot of questions, I got a bit agitated. And I felt like if he knew what was really going on, then he was going to make things a lot worse than they were."

"Did you really love Neeko?" I don't know why I asked the question but it seemed appropriate. This was heavy shit . . . and worse, it seemed as if Neeko and Katrina's relationship was built on a foundation of lies.

"Of course I loved Neeko. And I tried proving that to him every chance I got."

"Can I ask you another question?"

"I don't care. You can ask me anything." She continued to cry.

"Did you have anything to do with Neeko getting killed?"

Before Katrina answered, she broke down and really balled her eyes out. She made me think that I must've struck a nerve and hit a sore spot when I asked her that question. So I immediately stood up from my chair and embraced her. I wanted her to feel as if she could continue to confide in me and I wouldn't judge her. I rubbed her back in a circular motion. And then I told her that everything would be all right.

"No, it's not," she cried. "I lead Neeko and Bishop to their death just so I could save my own life."

"Did you do it because Duke threatened to kill you?"

She nodded. "Yeah, he threatened to kill me and the daughter I got by Neeko."

"But why?" I pressed the issue.

"Well, no one knew it but right after Duke got his hands on that ten million dollars, Neeko got into a bit of a money jam at the club, and since his credit wasn't that good, he asked me to go to my bank to see if I could get a personal loan. So I said okay. But after I filled out all the paperwork and gathered up all the documents they needed, those sons of bitches denied me. But I couldn't tell Neeko that because he was depending on me. And without him knowing, I went to Duke and got him to lend me the fifty grand Neeko and I needed to get everything back on track. Now me, of all people, should've known he wasn't giving that type of money up that easy. So after he made me sign a promissory note acknowledging that I would use this house as collateral since my name was on the deed with Neeko's, he made me sleep with him for old times' sake. I was sick to my stomach after I left him that night.

"Did Neeko ever found out?"

"Yeah, he found out about five months later when it was time for me to pay up," she began to explain. "I started taking a few hundred dollars here and there, so Neeko wouldn't notice. But then Duke started hanging out at the club and he'd harass me every chance he got. And when Neeko found out what he was doing, he stepped to Duke and it didn't end well. Duke told Neeko everything except for the fact that I fucked him and the part about my baby girl not being Neeko's child."

"I don't remember that. Was I working there then?" I wanted to know.

"No, you hadn't started working there yet. That happened like two months before you started."

"So, what did Neeko do?"

"He didn't do anything but convinced Duke to re-do the promissory note and swap the part about our house being the collateral and added the club instead."

"Oh, so that's why he used to be up there all the time. He had a legal stake in Magic City."

"Yep, that's why."

Trying to wrap my mind around this major bombshell Katrina dropped in my lap, it dawned on me that she never gave me the details about how she led Neeko to Duke. I knew I wouldn't be able to rest until she told me the truth. Not only that, I wanted to know if those two brothers who Bishop owed money to had anything to do with the club blowing up? So I asked her.

"No, that wasn't any of their doing," she replied. "Duke planned the whole thing. And he did it so he could collect his part of the insurance and get rid of Bishop at the same time."

"Did you know that Duke's new wife just went inside the club right after Bishop did?"

Katrina looked like she was shocked. She pressed her hand against her mouth. "No, I swear I didn't know that part. He didn't mention anything about her to me. All he said was that we needed to get rid of the club so we could collect the insurance money and that way he could pay back most of the money that he still owes to those brothers."

"Well, I hate to be the one to break it to you, but that slimy ass nigga sent his wife to her death. And it wouldn't surprise me if he did it to collect her insurance money as well."

"Oh my God! Lynise, what are we going to do? He might try to kill us next."

"I don't know about you but I don't plan to sit around and let him get me a second time."

"And neither do I," she said with fear dripping with every word. "But he told me that I can't go anywhere until I get my part of the insurance money from the club and sign the check over to him."

"Does Diamond know about the insurance scheme involving the club?"

"I don't think so. But even if he did tell her, he kept her doped up enough for her not to remember one day from the next."

"What do you think about them fucking around?"

"That's the thing, I don't think about her at all. She is a lost case. And she's a walking time bomb that's going to detonate any day now."

"Why do you think he's with her?"

"Duke has always had a thing for younger women. So if he can find him one who'd kiss his ass, massage his ego and stay inside one of his many properties all day so he can fuck them at his leisure, then he feels like he's gotten himself a winner."

"I didn't do any of that," I spoke up. I had to let Katrina know that I wasn't the type of chick to lay around and let a nigga dictate to me. That's what my mouth and emotions said but the truth be told, that was me to a certain extent. I wanted to think that I graduated from being the *complete fool* to a somewhat wise woman. Hence, that's why I was in the position I was in now. I grew up, I grew wise . . . and those factors alone made me a threat to the control freak named Duke Carrington.

"Well, if you didn't do it, then trust me, he had a dozen of them that did."

With all the comments Katrina made surrounding all

UNIQUE

the women Duke fucked with after their brief encounter made me wonder how she really felt when I started dating him. Okay, granted she popped up with his baby, so maybe she felt she still had some type of entitlement. But on the downside, she wasn't able to ever tell the world that he was her fucking baby daddy. I was anxious to know what went through her mind when she found out I moved into his spot at the Cosmopolitan building. So I asked her. That was me. If I wanted to know something, hell, the best thing to do was ask the damn question.

Before she answered me, she hesitated for a moment while she patted her eyes dry with the palm of her hands. Then she positioned her body so she could sit up straight in the chair. She acted like she had to get herself together. So I waited patiently. Finally, she said, "I'm gonna be honest and say that I was somewhat jealous at first, because you are very pretty. And when he made you quit working at the club, I really caught feelings because I felt like he was going to finally settle down. But right after you moved into the condo over in Pembroke, he started seeing the chick he later married. And that made me believe that he would never be faithful or treat any woman the way they deserve to be treated. So, I was happy about that."

"Did Duke ever promise you that you and him would be together?" I asked out of curiosity.

"No, he never mentioned anything about me and him being together as a couple, because I went into the relationship with him knowing what type of guy he was. Plus, I was still in love with Neeko. And he knew it."

"So why did it bother you when you found out about

CHEAPER *to* KEEP HER 2

him getting with other chicks?"

"Well, it didn't bother me like you think. See, the only time I would get upset is when shit wasn't going right with me and Neeko, and when I picked up the phone to call Duke, he would act like he didn't want to be bothered. Other than that, I was happy with the man I had. The only thing I wished I could change is the fact that I stopped fucking Duke without a condom. I mean, don't get me wrong, I'm glad I had my baby girl, but I just wished I would've done it with Neeko, and then I wouldn't be going through all this shit right now."

"Where are your girls now?"

"I shipped them out of town until I could come and get them."

"When is Neeko's funeral?"

"In three days."

"Are you going to bring them back for the funeral?"

"No. I can't let them see him in that casket like that."

"So, what are you going to do about Bishop's situation? Are you going to call his family?"

"I didn't want to tell you this, but I've already called and told them what happened?" she replied and then she got up from the kitchen chair. I thought she was going to pace the floor again, but she walked out of the kitchen altogether.

UNIQUE

GOING INTO BITCH MODE

I *was alone in the kitchen and extremely and jittery.*
I still didn't trust Katrina and why in the hell would she leave me alone. By the time I caught up with her, she was coming towards me in the hallway with her Blackberry in her hand. "Listen to this," she said and handed me the phone.

I put her phone against my ear and listened to the recording. "What the hell is going on down there? This is the second time you called my house and left me a message about one of my sons getting killed," I heard a woman roar. It was obvious she was extremely upset. "You better call me back as soon as you get this message. I need more answers." The woman continued to roar and then the recording stopped.

When the electronic voice prompted me to either press four to hear the message again or press the pound button to continue to the next message, I took the phone from my ear and handed it back to its owner. "I take it that's Bishop's and Neeko's mother?"

Katrina nodded while pressing the end button and

turned to walk back in the direction in which I was following her. She led me down the hall to the den area of her house. I took a seat on her leather sofa. She sat down next to me and placed her blackberry on the coffee table in front of us. "Are you going to call her back?" I asked her.

"Not right now," she replied.

"So what are we going to do now?"

Before Katrina had a chance to answer me, her cell phone started ringing. She picked it back up from the coffee table, looked at the caller ID screen and her face froze instantly. "Oh my God! It's Duke," she whispered.

Hearing Duke's name sent an eerie feeling and chills throughout my body. I started to tell her not to answer his call but I couldn't get my mouth to move. It wouldn't have made a difference because it was apparent she had already made her mind up. "Hello," she said.

I couldn't hear what he was saying but when Katrina replied to him by asking him if he was outside now, I nearly jumped out of my fucking skin. I panicked and abruptly got up from the sofa. Katrina stood to her feet as she pressed the end button and then she looked at me.

"He's outside for real?" I asked as paranoia spewed from my mouth. I wanted Katrina to tell me that I was hallucinating. Instead, she grabbed me instead and told me that I needed to hide. "But where?" I asked.

"Go upstairs and hide in my oldest daughter's bedroom," she instructed me as she lead me to the staircase that was not too far from where we were.

UNIQUE

Panic stricken, I ran up the staircase and when I reached the top of the stairs I didn't know which way to go. "Which room is it?" I asked her.

"The second door on the right," Katrina whispered as loud as she could. Then she vanished. I knew she didn't want to keep Duke waiting because it would definitely arouse suspicion and neither one of us wanted that.

When I entered into Katrina's daughter's bedroom I froze for brief second trying to figure out where would be a good place for me to hide. I looked at her daughter's bed and thought about hiding underneath it. However, when I got down on my knees to measure the space, I realized that my body would be too big to fit. So I jumped back up on my feet and dashed into the closet. There was very limited space with all the clothes and shoes this little girl had, but I made do and found a spot on the floor on the right side of the closet. I hid behind two very large Hello Kitty suitcases. And when I found a comfortable spot I sat with my back against the wall and wrapped my arms around my legs as I pressed my breast firmly against my knees. I knew I couldn't do anything else, so I sat there and said a silent prayer while I waited.

"Who you got in here?" I heard Duke ask Katrina. His tone was very authoritative and it sent shock waves through my eardrums. I became more scared than ever. I figured that it was a matter of time before he'd be pulling me out of this closet and killing me with his bare hands.

"Nobody," I heard Katrina reply. I could tell in her voice that she may have been more scared than I was.

"Bitch! You better not be lying to me!" Duke roared.

"I'm not," she assured him.

"Well, whose truck is that outside?" he pressed the issue.

"Remember when I told you this morning that Bishop was driving a suburban?"

"Yeah."

"Well, that's it."

"I thought he drove it to the club," he continued to press. From the way things looked in my eyes, it sounded like his statement was more of a question and he was waiting for Katrina to slip up and lie. Luckily for her she was quick on her feet.

"He did drive it to the club," I heard her respond. "But right after the fire broke out I drove it out of the parking lot and parked it across the street where the barbershop and beauty salon is."

"So how did it get here?" he persisted.

"I had it towed."

"Well, where is the towing receipt?" he came back at her. At first Katrina was on a roll. Every question Duke threw her way, she came back with a plausible answer. But for some reason he must've felt that she was lying in some shape or fashion, because he kept probing her with one question after another.

"I told the guy not to give me one. I mean would it have made sense for me to get a receipt? Look at what just happened tonight. We don't need a paper trail at this point in the game," she finally explained.

Duke didn't answer right off. There was complete silence for at least a minute and a half before he responded. "You better not be lying to me! Because if I found out that you have, then you're going to be lying in a grave

UNIQUE

next to my wife." Then I heard footsteps as they passed the staircase.

Fuck, if he is this scary, I didn't want to fuck with the brothers who had him scared as shit.

Now I had to admit that I didn't see Katrina coming out of this one. I knew she was about to get herself crossed up and the fucked up part about it was I wasn't going to be able to help her. I swear, if it were me, I would've thrown her ass underneath the bus and told him exactly where she was. Because when it was all said and done, everybody was going to look out for their own ass.

Meanwhile, they were moving about through the house. That's when I realized I heard three sets of footprints. But to be perfectly sure, I remained quiet so I could continue to hear everything that was going on downstairs.

I couldn't say for sure but it sounded like Katrina and Duke were in the den, because their conversation wasn't as clear as it was before. I damn near had to hold my breath in order to hear them really good.

Duke basically ran the entire conversation. He was giving Katrina more instructions than anything. I hoped and prayed he wouldn't be here very long because my legs weren't going to cooperate with me if I stayed in this position for more than twenty to thirty minutes. There was limited space for me to readjust my legs so this was only a temporary fix. Thank God I had on a watch to keep track of time. If I didn't have one on I would be up shit's creek without a paddle or a hope of a prayer to save my ass.

I had only been sitting for five minutes and it seemed

CHEAPER *to* KEEP HER 2

like I had been here for an eternity. So many thoughts were running through my mind and I couldn't figure out how to line every one of them up.

Duke's grimy ass was at the center of it all. I hadn't laid eyes on him since I've gotten out of jail, but I could see his face as clear as the day. He had such a negative impact on people's lives that the remnants from his wrath never left a person's mind. I mean, this guy was so evil and sadistic it really was scary. I had fucked a lot of men in my lifetime but I never seen a man like him ever. He was so fucking charismatic on the surface. But deep down in his soul and heart, he had this sick obsession of seeing people down on their knees begging him to spare their lives. People's weakness fueled his adrenaline which was a sad way to live. If I was fortunate to walk out of this situation tonight, then I was going to show that motherfucker who the fuck I really am!

Even though I thought his evil ass was the Devil's son reincarnated.

WHO'S BEHIND DOOR #1

*T*wenty-five minutes had passed and Duke showed no sign he had plans to leave anytime soon.

My legs had become numb and my fucking bladder had filled up to its capacity. I knew it wouldn't be much longer before I exploded and pissed all over myself. Once again I called on the Good Lord and asked Him if he would please speak to Duke's heart by giving him a revelation so he could carry his ass home or back to his Devil's lair. But it was evident he wouldn't be able to hear Him because Duke served the Darkness Below. And since there was nothing else for me to do, I continued to sit there and hoped I'd be able to hold out just a little bit longer.

"Is there anymore Coronas in the refrigerator?" Duke asked.

"Yeah, they're three left," she replied.

"Well, go in there and get me and Chris one," he instructed her.

Immediately after I heard Duke instruct Katrina to go into the kitchen and bring him and Chris both a bottle of Corona, I felt a knot in my stomach. Not only was it revealed that I was right about there being another person in the house, but it also potentially meant that something may jump off. And the thought of that really made my stomach sick all over again.

Chris was Duke's right-hand man, so he operated under Duke's command. He was the massa's puppet. There was a lot of buzz while I was in jail that Chris was the one who actually pulled the trigger and killed Neeko. I wondered if it bothered Katrina to have the man who shot and killed her husband lounging on her fucking living room furniture. There's absolutely no way that motherfucker would be in my house after he shot and killed my man. And to make matters worse, Duke had her in the kitchen getting that animal a fucking beer. If it were me, I would have poured his beer into a glass and spit in it. And if I wanted to get gangster on their asses, I'd have poison both of those bastards and let them die a slow death.

"What's taking you so long to bring us back the motherfucking beer?" Duke yelled. If he had yelled any louder he'd probably shatter every glass in the house. That's how ferocious he sounded.

"I'm coming now" Katrina assured him. I heard her footsteps as she scrambled down the hallway. Hell, I wondered for a quick second if she had put some shit in their beers. That shit would have been righteous if she did.

"Where is your bathroom?" I heard Chris ask.

UNIQUE

"In the hallway by the kitchen," Katrina replied.

Seconds later, I heard heavier footsteps as they walked down the hallway and then I heard a door close. But as quickly as he closed it, he opened it right back up. "Where is your other bathroom?" he yelled down the hallway.

I heard Katrina scramble back down the hall towards him. "What's wrong with this bathroom?" she wanted to know.

"The light doesn't work. It must be blown," he told her.

I listened intensely. Something wasn't right. I hope it was just my imagination.

"Okay. Just stay right there and I'll run upstairs to get you a new one," she replied and then I heard her footsteps as she hurried towards the staircase. But before she was able to climb one step, Duke stopped her in her tracks.

"Wait! Hold up a fucking minute!" he commanded.

"What? What's wrong?" she asked and then complete silence filled the air until I heard another set of footsteps. And when I heard Duke's voice again, I could tell he was standing directly in front of her.

"What the fuck is up with you? You've been jumpy since I walked into this goddamn house!" he snapped.

"Nothing's wrong with me," she told him. But I heard the fear in her voice and I knew he heard it too. At that point, I got scared as shit for Katrina. Was she a dead woman?

"You're not hiding anything from me are you?" Duke said with venom and vile in his voice.

"Of course not," she began to say. "Have I ever hid

anything from you?"

"There's a first time for everything," he replied as quickly as the words were out of her mouth.

Chris must've lost his patience because he didn't waste any time by telling her not to worry about getting another light bulb for the bathroom, because he was going to use the bathroom upstairs. I waited for Katrina to respond but she didn't say a word. I wished like hell there was some way I could see what was going on. But since I was stuck in the back of Katrina's daughter's closet I shifted my eardrums in full force.

"Want me to get a light bulb while I'm up here?" I heard Chris ask. By this time, he was climbing the staircase.

"Nah, you don't have to worry about it. If I told you where they were, you still wouldn't be able to find them. Especially with all the mess I got piled up in the hallway linen closet."

"A'ight," Chris replied. As I listened in on their conversation, I heard Chris go into the bathroom, which had to be next to the bedroom I was in, because it sounded like he was only a few feet away. And when he started pissing in the toilet I nearly freaked out, because if he had the slightest inclination I was in the next room, he'd serve me up on a platter to Duke and then he'd torture me while Duke watched. So I held my breath because it felt like I was breathing too loud. I couldn't take the chance of being dragged out of this closet.

Right after that bastard emptied his bladder, I heard him flush the toilet stool and before he exited the bathroom, I heard his cell phone ring. He answered after the first ring. "Hello," I heard him say and then he fell silent. "I'm in the beach right now," he continued, but then he fell silent again.

"I don't know how long I'm gonna be," he snapped. From the way his conversation was going, it seemed as if he was getting a little agitated. "Look, Tiffany, don't be asking me a whole bunch of fucking questions. When I do what I came out here to do then I'll be home," he continued and then he stopped talking altogether. The next thing I heard was his footsteps as they passed the room I was hiding in. The moment I heard him walking back down the staircase, I stopped holding my breath and exhaled.

Once I regained my composure, I couldn't help but recall Chris's phone conversation. It was obvious that his disrespectful ass was talking to his wife or possibly his baby mama. But in any case, he mentioned to her that he had something to take care of for Duke. So I wondered what that could be. First, I thought about the possibility that Duke had Chris were here to eliminate Katrina from the equation. But then I thought that it wouldn't make sense to do that. According to Katrina, Duke needed her around to get her part of the insurance money. So what else could it be?

I racked my brain trying to figure out what was Duke's motive for coming here and bringing Chris along. And when I couldn't come up with a solid answer, I decided to shift that situation to the back of my mind until I was able to come to a conclusion in this matter.

Once again, I looked down at my wristwatch and noticed I had been sitting in this same position for over an hour now. And with no signs that Duke, nor Chris, was leaving anytime soon, I pressed my luck and decided to take a chance by sneaking into the bathroom. I knew that I was playing a very deadly game. But I figured if I tip-toed out of the room and into the hallway, then I could get away with it without getting caught. I mean, what other choice did I have? I didn't want to pee on myself because you've got to remember that adults' urine is a lot stronger than children's. So why bring the heat to myself when it could be avoided?

It took me almost five whole minutes to get up from the floor. My legs and feet were super duper numb. So when I stood up on my feet, I leaned up against the wall in the closest to get some of the feeling back and let the blood began to circulate through my veins. A few minutes later, I got up the gumption to take the first step. There wasn't much room to move around in the closet. You could take two to three steps and you were in or out. So after I stepped around the two Hello Kitty suitcases, I grabbed a hold of the doorknob and turned it very quietly. I couldn't tell you why but I held my breath again. I was breathing so hard, it felt like as soon as I walked out of this closet and into the hallway, they'd hear me. And I couldn't let that happen.

Thankfully enough, I was able to open the closet door without making a sound. My next quest was to make it out of the bedroom as quickly and as quietly as I possibly could. So right after I took the first couple of steps, I stopped because my gut feeling told me to prepare for an escape exit if all else failed. And that's exactly what I intended to do.

UNIQUE

The bedroom window was on the opposite side of the room so I tiptoed over to it and wasted no time trying to find the latch that would help me raise it up. While I prepared an escape route, I heard bits and pieces of Duke's and Chris's conversation. Fortunately, they weren't talking about killing or the death of another human being. They were discussing how they were going to make other moves to secure the rest of the money he owed those two cats Katrina mentioned to me earlier. So while they were putting a plan in motion, I had found the latch and began to lift it very gently. It was moving smoothly until I had gotten it halfway up and then it acted like it didn't want to move anymore. Frustrated and scared at the same time, I tried to use a little more force behind my push and when I did, the window made a screeching sound. From that very moment, you could hear a pen drop. That's how quiet it had gotten. And from there, my heart leaped out my fucking chest because I knew it was a matter of seconds before I would be faced with Duke and Chris.

I stood there about to piss all over my clothes when I heard footsteps running up the staircase. I figured if I stood there any longer, I'd be their next victim. So I forced the window up more and then I kicked the screen out with my feet. But when I climbed up on the window ledge I couldn't help but notice that if I tried to jump down onto the ground I would surely break my fucking legs. But I couldn't just stand there and let those niggas fuck me up so I raced towards the bedroom door and hurried up and locked it. I figured by me locking it, it would give me a little more time to figure out how to climb out of this window without crippling myself.

CHEAPER *to* KEEP HER 2

With my heart pounding like a racehorse I climbed back on the ledge and then I eased my way through the window, sliding out on my stomach. And as soon as I had gotten halfway through, I heard two gunshots and then the bedroom door flew open. My eyes damn near popped out of my head when Chris burst into the room with Duke in tow. I could tell in their eyes that they were shocked to see me. Chris aimed his gun at me. "It's Lynise!" he yelled.

"Shoot that bitch in the head!" Duke instructed him and Chris followed through by letting off two more rounds. BOOM! BOOM!

I saw the sparks from the barrel of the gun after he fired both shots. I knew I didn't want to die. But I also knew that I didn't want to let go of the window ledge and drop down twenty feet to the ground. "God, show me what to do," I said and then I closed my eyes. And without given it anymore thought, I let go of the window ledge.

God be with me and please, stay with me.

UNIQUE

ANOTHER ONE BITES THE DUST

If only I could fly, I thought, as I let go of the ledge and felt the wind beneath me.

It was a matter of seconds before my body fell into a bush with sharp limbs. The limbs cut through my skin really bad. But I couldn't complain. The bush also was a lifesaver, because it broke my fall. Lucky for me the entire backyard was pitch-black. So after I rolled myself out of the bush I scrambled to my feet. But I was only able to move a few feet before Chris started shooting his gun again. Duke nor Chris was able to see me but it didn't stop the damn fool from pointing his pistol in every location of the backyard.

"Do you see her?" Duke yelled.

"No, I don't see her anywhere," Chris told him.

"Come on, let's hurry up and get her before she gets away." Duke instructed.

I was scraped up pretty bad. But knowing that they were on their way downstairs, allowed me to block out all the pain I was feeling so I could use my strength to get out of there. Katrina's backyard was pretty big. And it was fenced in. The fence was made with iron and it was only six feet tall, which wasn't hard for me to climb over. I was breathing so hard, I was panting. By the time I reached the other side I saw Chris running directly towards me. He came from the front of the house, so I had no choice but to turn and run in the opposite direction. I had no idea where I was going. And the fact that it was extremely dark outside prevented me from planning a better escape. All I knew was that I needed to run because my life depended on it.

It seemed like the further I ran, the shorter of the distance Chris had to catch up with me. "When I get my hands on you bitch, I am going to choke your mother-fucking ass out," I heard him threaten me from behind.

I thought he would've fired more gunshots at me. But for some reason, he didn't. And since he hadn't, I figured that maybe he ran out of bullets from shooting blindly at me in the backyard. Whether I was right or wrong, I was determined not to let him catch me. Not tonight nor any other night. So I mustered up every inch of strength I had to pick up speed. My heart raced at a faster speed than my legs as I continued to prevent this maniac from catching me. I hope Chris's big ass wasn't in the kind of shape that I was.

A couple of times I tripped when my feet landed on uneven ground. I didn't know this at first, but Katrina's house and her neighbor's houses were built around a

man-made lake. I contemplated jumping in the lake but I
was afraid it might've been too deep for me to swim in.
And I definitely didn't want to drown. Then I thought
drowning would be a better way to die than fatal gunshots
wounds.

It seemed as if Chris had chased me for at least a mile
but when I looked back I saw the bedroom light from Katrina's house and the distance between me and her house
was less than a quarter of a mile. "Lord," please help
me!" I prayed underneath my breath. I needed God more
now than any other time in my life. I hoped the Good
Lord heard me and didn't ignore my pleas.

It seemed like Chris had no plans of giving up. I even
noticed he was getting closer to me than I thought. I figured if I kept running at the speed I was traveling, then
he'd eventually catch up to me.

Besides the sound of running feet, I'm sure I heard
Chris breathing really hard. He was breathing so hard he
could barely catch his breath. Although he seemed a little
winded, that bastard showed no other sign that he would
slow his big ass down. So without much more thought, I
did the unthinkable. I dipped through a set of gigantic
trees and then I made a quick left turn towards the lake
and dove straight in. The immediate splash from the water was loud enough for the neighbors to hear. So I was
hoping it would dawn on at least one of them to investi-
gate it.

"You motherfucking bitch!" Chris screamed. I could
tell he was pissed that I had jumped into the lake. And
when I looked back, I noticed that he'd stopped in his
tracks. My heart skipped a beat when I realized he hadn't

jumped in the water behind me. I wanted to stop swimming but my mind wouldn't let me. I knew I had to get as far away from Duke and Chris as quickly as I could.

When I looked back again, I noticed Chris had disappeared from where he was originally standing. A new level of panic shot through my entire body. I didn't know whether to keep swimming to the other side of the lake or turn back. Either way, I wanted to avoid Chris from catching me.

The water in the lake wasn't as deep as I thought it was, but the temperature was freezing cold. And I knew that very soon I would need to get out of it. Without making a lot of noise I decided to move about in the lake. Instead of swimming to the opposite side of the lake, I swam to the East side. I figured if Chris and Duke were looking for me, they'd wait for me directly on the opposite side in which I entered. I stopped a couple of times before I was able to exit the lake. For one, I was extremely exhausted from all of the running I had done before I jumped into the water. And two, it seemed like the more speed I put behind my swimming, the louder the splashes got so I had to slow my pace. It bothered the hell out of me that I couldn't see a thing around me. I could see the light from Katrina's daughter's room was still on, but that was it.

I thought about screaming for help at one point. But then I figured that wouldn't be a smart move, because what if no one hears me but Duke and Chris? I'd really be a dead bitch then. So after taking a couple of swimming breaks, I finally got up the nerve to swim back to land.

I said another silent prayer and exited the water quietly. I got down on my knees and crawled behind a tree that was near someone's backyard. I waited there for a moment, while on high alert. My heart was beating like a racehorse but I did my best to remain calm. A couple of times I jumped because I heard crackling sounds around me. But when I looked a little closer, I realized there were a couple of squirrels playing around, so I exhaled. I knew I wasn't out of harm's way yet and that's why I kept my guard up. After being on my knees for at least a good five minutes, I stood up, but hunched down so I couldn't be spotted if Chris was indeed waiting for me to reveal myself.

Being that it was extremely dark it became impossible for me to plan an escape route. I was able to still see Katrina's house because no one ever turned off the bedroom lights. Suddenly my actions hit me. During all of the excitement, I hadn't thought about Katrina. Now I wondered what kind of turmoil she was in. I knew how Duke operated so there was no question in my mind that he was beating the hell out of her. I knew his ass wasn't going to spare her any leniency because she had me hiding upstairs in her daughter's room. Trust me, he was making her tell him why I was there and what we were talking about before he arrived at the house. Knowing that she threw her own man and his brother underneath the bus, I knew she sung like a bird when he questioned her about me.

I couldn't blame her. After all, my new motto was the same motto as most of America, "survivor of the fittest." I could only apologize to her in my mind.

It wouldn't surprise me if she lied and told Duke that I followed her to her house and how I knew where she lived. Either way it wouldn't matter to me, because her life was in the palm of his hands and mine wasn't. Well, at least, for now it wasn't.

Once I felt like the coast was clear, I tried my luck and maneuvered my way out of the darkness surrounding Katrina's neighborhood. With every move I made I had to look back and see if I were being followed. I was disappointed no one had called the cops after hearing gunshots and me splashing around in the lake. This wasn't the 'hood. This was a nicer part of the beach and they didn't suppose to go for that shit out here. Or that's the lie we in the 'hood suppose to believe.

When I got at least a half of mile away from Katrina's house, that's when I knew Chris had turned back and gone back to Katrina's house. Drenched from head to toe from that nasty lake water, my clothes clung to my body like a bad habit and I wanted nothing else but to get out of them. I had nowhere to go to do just that. And even if I did, I didn't have a spare change of clothes, so once again I was ass out. One part of me wanted to just scream out loud and ask God why me? Why was I going through all of this turmoil? I also wanted to ask God how was this all going to end? I knew He was the only one who knew what was around the next corner. And the fact I didn't know nearly drove me crazy.

I looked down at my watch and noticed it had not only stopped, but it also had water damage. I sighed heavily. I felt like if it wasn't one thing, then it was damn sure another. And since I had no way of knowing what time it was, I bit the bullet and kept it moving down side streets to prevent from being seen, just in case Duke sent Chris back out to look for me.

I wished I had a chance to go back and get Bishop's truck. I was at least ten or fifteen miles away from the downtown area of Virginia Beach, so I knew I wouldn't be able to get there on foot. I also knew it would be impossible to get to Bishop's truck. If Chris wasn't out here looking for me, I knew he was certainly keeping his eyes on that truck.

And for the first time I wondered if revenge was worth my life . . . or worse, my death.

FUCK EVERYBODY

*O*nly a fool wouldn't change their fortune.
I didn't know who said that but they were right.
And that's why I had to see this through. That was the only way to change my fortune—I had to see this son-of-a-bitch in jail or dead.

I practically dragged myself a half of mile before I was able to come upon a gas station. It was more or less one of those convenient stores with a couple of old ass gas pumps outside and a store full of Arabs who posed as the owners. When I walked inside, everybody in the store, including the customers turned around and stared at me like their fucking minds was going bad. I dismissed all of them with a funky ass expression and proceeded to the counter. I knew everyone probably wondered why I was soaked and wet when it hasn't rained in the last twenty-four hours. But I couldn't worry about them. I had other shit on my mind.

"You got a phone I can use?" I asked one of the two

men that were standing behind the counter.

The one nearest to the register said, "Sorry, we don't have a public phone."

"But I got an emergency. I need to call somebody so they can come and get me," I expressed with urgency.

But he insisted that he wasn't about to let me use the store's telephone. I became extremely frustrated. I mean, he saw how I looked, so it wasn't hard to tell that I needed some type of assistance. And as bad as I wanted to curse him out, I held back all my anger and suggested that if he didn't want me to use his phone, then could he dial the number for me. I further explained that I had just escaped from this man who was trying to kill me.

"I'm sorry but I can't help you," he replied. "Go outside and use the pay phone," he continued and pointed towards the door.

When he pulled that stunt I nearly lost it and instantly retaliated, "If I had money I would've used the fucking pay phone outside, you idiot! Y'all come here from your country with your little bit ass money so you can set up shop and overcharge us black folks with all that expired shit you got on those nasty ass shelves. Y'all think y'all got all the sense in the world but you don't. Y'all ain't shit! Y'all ain't nothing but fake ass Muslims trying to get rich off of us. But this place ain't last long 'cause I'm gonna get my boyfriend to blow this shit up. You fucking has-beens!"

Immediately after storming out of the convenience store, I marched across the parking lot. I was damn near to tears when this guy approached me from behind. "Yo' Shorty, was that shit you said true about a nigga trying to kill you?"

I turned around and looked into the eyes of this five feet eleven cat with a shiny bald head. I started to get sarcastic with his ass for asking me that stupid ass question but once again I held my tongue. Primarily because he might let me use that Blackberry he had attached to his hip. I hesitated for a moment and then I said, "Nah, I was kidding. I only said it to see if he would let me use his phone."

The guy laughed. "Yo' sweetheart, you are mad funny!" he commented.

But I didn't think the shit was funny so I didn't laugh with him. He caught on really quick. "Yo', my bad! I'm sorry for laughing at you."

"Do you mind if I use your phone?" I cut to the chase. I really didn't want to engage in any small talk with this guy. All I wanted was to use his phone and that was it.

The guy took his Blackberry from his holster and handed it to me. "Yeah, sure you can use it."

I took the phone from him and tried one more time to see if I could get my ex, Devin, on the phone. But once again that tired ass nigga refused to answer his line. I knew before I even dialed his number that I wasn't going to be able to talk to him calling from this unknown number. He was really big on sending unknown numbers to his voicemail. And the fact that his voicemail was full, I couldn't even leave him a message. I was so frustrated, I just ended the call and handed this guy his phone back.

I sighed heavily as I stood before him. I couldn't think of anyone else to call. I didn't even have a place that I could go to. So I stood there and wondered to myself what my next move would be.

"If you need a ride somewhere I'm sure my cousin wouldn't mind dropping you off," he told me.

"Where's your cousin now?" I asked.

He pointed to an old mid-size van that was tricked out with a white and silver flip-flop colored exterior paint, tinted windows and a set of chrome rims. "He's right there sitting in the driver seat of that caravan."

I frowned when I checked out this guy's cousin. From where I was standing his cousin had to be at least fifty years old. He looked more like his father than his cousin. But I rolled with it. I mean, who was I to say how they were related. I was in a bad place and I had no other options, so I took this guy up on his offer and decided to accompany them.

On our way towards the van I asked him, what was his name? He told me his name was Leroy and his cousin's name was Tyrone. They also didn't live too far from the convenience store. The he switched the conversation around and asked me how did I get so wet? By this time I was standing outside of the van with the sliding door pulled back. Leroy was inside trying to find something for me to sit on, so I wouldn't saturate their backseat with my wet clothes.

I started to tell him the truth about me jumping into the lake but then I decided against it. I was like the military—they didn't have a *need to know*. So I fabricated a story about being thrown into a pool and I was so mad at the person who done it, that I just simply left and didn't look back. I sensed he believed me because he commented that he would never do something like that. Then

CHEAPER *to* KEEP HER 2

he started talking about something else.

While I was waiting for him to lay a cover or something on the backseat, his older cousin, who looked like he could be his father, started flirting with me.

"See, if you stop messing around with those young boys and get with a man like me, then I can show you how you supposed to be treated."

Leroy burst into laughter. "Come on down, Tyrone, that lady ain't in the mood for your old school pickup lines," he commented.

"They may be old school, but they are real!" old school Tyrone replied.

Any other woman would've laughed and gave the old man a nice kiss on the cheek for his efforts, but he chose the wrong night and the wrong girl to flirt with, especially after all I had been through in the last ten hours.

When Leroy grabbed my hand to help me climb into the van, I saw the headlights of a small sports car pull up on the other side of the van. My heart nearly jumped out of my fucking chest, because I knew how the engine idled on Duke's Porshe. And since I hadn't heard anyone else's car that sounded like his whip, I knew it had to be him. I pushed Leroy out of the way and rushed inside of his cousin's van without his assistance.

"Are you all right?" he questioned me.

I wanted to tell him that the owner of the car was after me. But I change my mind. I didn't know these men so I couldn't risk them turning me over to Duke. Nor could I risk Duke following me once he figured out where I was. So I played it off and acted like I was just a little anxious to sit down.

UNIQUE

"Are you sure?" Leroy pressed the issue.

"Yes, I'm sure," I assured him.

"Boy, sit down. The young lady said she was fine. Now, let's get out of here," Tyrone spoke up.

Leroy took his advice and slammed the door shut. And right after he got into the front passenger seat, Tyrone put the van in reverse and proceeded to back out of the parking lot.

Fortunately for me no one could see inside the van. But I could see out and while Tyrone was backing out of the parking lot I finally got a chance to see that it was in fact Duke's Porsche. The butterflies in my stomach started jumping around rapidly. My heart started beating like crazy too. All I wanted at that very moment was for Tyrone to get out of this place quickly. I'm guessing he was taking his merry time to get out of another patron's way because someone in a car behind us started blowing their horn.

"Can you hurry up and get that shit out of the way!" I heard the road raged driver scream.

Everyone in the parking lot turned and looked in our direction. And when the passenger side door opened and Chris got out of it, he looked back at the van too.

I swear I was about to freak out. I wanted to throw up right where I was sitting. These two guys had no idea what was going on and they wouldn't be able to grasp the amount of danger they could possibly be in if Duke and Chris knew I was with them. So to prevent these innocent men from getting hurt I knew I had to tell them something. It wasn't going to be the full truth, but it was going to be something really close.

CHEAPER *to* KEEP HER 2

"Hey, listen up guys, my boyfriend just got out of that silver Porsche right there. Now if you don't hurry up and get me out of here, he might suspect that I'm in here with y'all and try to drag me out of here," I twisted the truth.

Leroy spoke up first. "That lame looking motherfucker right there is your boyfriend?"

"Yeah, so we need to hurry up and leave."

"Fuck that! We ain't gotta leave! And he ain't gonna put his fucking hands on you either," Leroy continued.

"Look, I'm not one to judge, now he may look lame but he carries a big ass gun and he's not afraid to use it. So let's be smart and not play the hero," I warned him.

Apparently Cousin Tyrone took heed because he put his van in the drive position and sped out of the parking lot like he had just smoked some crack. He almost drove into the ditch when he made a left turn to get on to the next street.

"Leroy can act like he's a gangsta all he wants, but he's going to do that shit in his own car and on his own time," Tyrone commented after he got control of his van.

I let out a long sigh and then I laid my head against the headrest while Leroy and Tyrone went back and forth about how the situation with Chris should've been handled.

I started to jump into their conversation but Tyrone held his ground so my presence wasn't needed. He laid down plenty of scenarios where Leroy could've gotten hurt really bad, especially behind something that could've been avoided. "People these days are crazy," Tyrone began. "I've seen guys who'll kill you behind ten dollars. Now I know that is downright insane. But I ain't got time for that foolishness. I believe that this younger generation is possessed with demons because in all the days of my life I ain't ever seen so many young folk kill each other like they do today. So Leroy you better start acting like you got some damn sense. That mess you tried to involve yourself in tonight, can't ever happen again, especially if you with me."

Leroy tried to interject a few times but Tyrone wasn't having it. He made it perfectly clear that he wasn't happy with Leroy's actions. And I agreed. If we had more older men trying to teach young men like Tyrone than maybe the graveyards wouldn't be filled to capacity with younger black men. When I thought that, I thought about Neeko and Bishop, and the sadness of it all.

After Tyrone laid down the law to his baby cousin, he looked through his rearview mirror and asked me where he was dropping me off?

The first thing that came out of my mouth was, "2111 Bazemore Avenue."

"Where is that?" he asked me.

"It's in Norfolk," I told him.

"What part of Norfolk?"

"It's right off Military Highway near the Wal-mart," I replied and then I thought to myself, was I making the right choice by taking a trip over to Devin's apartment even though I hadn't been invited? I guess I would soon find out.

CHEAPER *to* KEEP HER 2

PUSSY FOR SALE

*S*ince the beginning of time, a woman has had to do what a woman has to do.

In the little bit of time it took for Mr. Tyrone to drive me to Devin's apartment, it felt like my clothes were starting to dry. Not that it made any different, because I still looked like shit. But the fact that I would soon be in dry clothes made me feel just a tad bit better.

The old man pulled slowly into the apartment complex where Devin resided. I immediately noticed his car was parked in his normal parking spot, so I go a little excited. I knew I was only minutes away from getting out of these wet ass clothes and into something dry. Not to mention that I'd be able to sleep in a warm bed. Shit, and the way I felt after running, ducking and dodging fucking bullets, if he held me right, I'd give him some pussy just for GP. And who knows, I could possibly let him eat my pussy too. After being in jail with those carpet munching chicks, I was desperately in the need of some licking and sticking. Hell, Bishop would've gotten it first if Katrina wouldn't have set him up to get killed. So I had to keep it moving and Devin was the next best thing. Hopefully, he was in the mood.

Before I got out of the van, I thanked them both for giving me a ride. I expressed how grateful I was and promised them that I would never forget them. Leroy tried to get me to give him a number so he'd be able to contact me but I told him I didn't have a phone number to give him. I'm sure he didn't believe me, but hey what can I say? Tyrone insisted on waiting in the parking lot until I got inside of Devin's apartment safely. But I assured him that I was fine and sent them on their way.

After they drove away, I realized that it probably would've been a good idea for them to stay until I got Devin to open up his door. I mean, it would be just my luck if I found out he decided to jump in the car with someone else and headed out on the streets for a few hours. Before departing Tyrone's van, I noticed the clock on his dashboard. It was a few minutes past midnight. So I crossed my fingers and hoped Devin was home.

I climbed up to the second floor and walked about one hundred feet from the staircase entryway to get to his front door, which was the sixth door on the right. My heartbeat pumped a little faster than normal. I guess it was because I didn't know how he would react after he opened the door and saw me standing there. I took a deep breath and hoped for the best.

I rung the doorbell a few times and when I didn't get an answer, I started knocking on his door. I wasn't count-ing but I believe I knocked every bit of twelve times. I even called out his name a few times but I still got no answer. The likelihood of me getting inside of his apartment tonight became very grim. Frustration and depression began to weigh me down. I felt like I had fifty pound dumbbells on my shoulders. I just wanted to ball up into a knot and roll back down the flight of steps I had just ascended.

I mean, what else could go wrong tonight?

I had nowhere to go. The hotel was off limits because of my unknown stalker. I was forced to leave Katrina's house because my life was in danger. Diamond's apartment was also off limits because she was now my adversary and now Devin's place was unavailable because he was nowhere to be found.

"Why in the fuck did I let those guys leave me?" I asked myself. And instead of answering my own question, I shook my head in disbelief and began to walk away from Devin's front door. When I got halfway down the hallway, I heard clicking sounds. I stopped in my tracks and turned back around. It sounded as if the unlocking door was Devin's. I waited and out popped his head. I let out a sigh of relief and ran towards him.

"I am so glad you're home," I told him.

Wearing only a pair of boxers, he acted like he wasn't happy to see me. I tried to dismiss his expression, but he didn't let me off that easy and said, "How you get over here?"

"I got a ride," I told him as I moved a little closer towards him.

He barricaded himself between the door and the door seal. I could tell he was trying to prevent me from seeing past him. "Why didn't you call me before you came over here?" His questions continued.

By now, I knew coming here was a bad move on my part. But I didn't have anywhere else to turn. "Look, Devin, I did call you but you didn't answer your phone," I explained.

"You must've called me from some unknown number?"

"Yeah, I called you from a couple of numbers. But let's not get into that. Right now, I need a place to lay my head tonight," I told him.

Before he was able to respond I heard a woman's voice say, 'baby, who's at the front door?' And then, she walked up behind him and looked over his shoulder. I could only see her face and I have to admit she was very pretty. But her facial expression turned sour as soon as she got one long look at me. "What the fuck happened to you?" she growled.

"None of your motherfucking business!" I snapped. I mean, how dare this bitch ask me what the fuck happened to me? She didn't know me from a can of paint. And because she was laying up in this nigga's house, she felt like she was obligated to question me. Hell nah, she better get back in her place, especially with the way I was feeling.

Before she could get another word in, Devin pushed her back from the door. "Kim, take your ass back in the room and stay there until I get there," he instructed.

I cracked a smile because I was proud that he had the balls to stand up for me. When we dated in the past, he would let all of his side chicks disrespect me at the drop of a hat. But today, I saw a changed man. "Look, Lynise," he began, "tonight is not a good night for you to be here."

"Devin, I don't care about her because I am not here for that. You can have twelve bitches in your room for all I care. All I need is a place to lay my head tonight and as soon as the morning comes, I will be out of here."

Devin stood there and thought to himself for a couple of seconds. He looked like he was about to stick to his guns and send me on my way. But I couldn't let that happen, so I began to plead my case.

"Devin, look at me. I am so tired. My clothes are soaked and wet right now. I have absolutely nowhere else to go. So please don't make me walk back in these streets tonight," I begged. "I promise, if you give me one of your T-shirts and a pair of your shorts to wear, I will hop on the sofa and you won't hear a peep out of me."

He thought for another second or two, and then he stepped back from his door. "Come on, but the first time you try some shit you're gonna have to leave," he warned me.

Happy about his decision, I damn near jumped into his arms. But I thanked him instead. "Thank you so much, Devin. Believe me, I'm going straight to sleep."

After he let me into the house, he closed the front door and locked it. All the lights in the apartment were off so I was standing in the dark, waiting for him to give me further instructions. "Wait right here," he said and then he disappeared.

I heard him as he made his way down the hallway. And immediately after he entered into his bedroom, he hit the light switch, turned the light on and then closed the door.

"Whatcha' doing?" his girl, Kim, didn't hesitate to ask.

"Just be quiet," he cut her off.

"I know you ain't gonna let her stay here tonight?" she continued to question him. But he didn't say word, so I think he put her ass on ignore.

"Oh, so now you gon' ignore me 'cause you got some other bitch in your house? Devin, don't make me put my clothes on and leave!" she ranted.

He continued to ignore her.

"Do you hear me?" she snapped. "I promise you that if you let her stay here I am going home," she continued to threaten him.

"Well, carry your ass home. I don't give a fuck!" he snapped back and then he walked back out of his bedroom and slammed the door. He stormed back down the hallway like he was pissed. So I played the innocent role and acted like I was eternally grateful. Well, actually, I was grateful so I made sure he knew it.

While he was handing me some of his clothes to change into, I heard yelling at the top of Kim's voice. And boy was she angry.

"I can't believe that motherfucka gon' get cute because he got another bitch in his house," she ranted. "And then on top of that, he gon' talk shit and tell me I can leave when he done already got the pussy. Now how trifling is that? But it's all right, that motherfucka gon' wished he didn't put that bitch before me."

"I'm sorry for all the trouble I caused," I told him,

even though I could care less. Devin was the type of nigga that didn't give a fuck about no one but himself. This was the way he was. Too bad she was just now seeing it. But I saw it firsthand not too long after we started dating. I guess this was my way of getting some get back and it felt really good.

"Don't worry about her. She's just talking shit! She'll be all right in the morning."

"Oh, so all I'm doing is talking shit, huh?" she roared after she walked into the living room.

Devin and I both turned around in her direction. I couldn't see her face clearly. But I could see her body movement. "Didn't I tell you not to come in here with all that drama?" Devin said.

"Fuck you nigga! I ain't the one causing the fucking drama!" she yelled back. "You're the one letting some random chick come up in here like she owns the place."

"Didn't I tell you to shut the fuck up?" he screamed.

Appalled by his disrespect, Kim flicked on the light switch. At that very moment everyone was able to see each other. She was completely dressed and she had her handbag in the palm of her left hand. She had her hair pulled back into a ponytail and she was dressed in a cute little fitted skirt with a semi-see-through dated strapless top. She sort of looked like Rhianna but with a little more weight. She looked as if she could be a stripper. Knowing the type of women Devin liked, it wouldn't have surprised me if she was.

"Nigga, do I look like I'm one of your kids?" she spat. "You don't be telling me to shut the fuck up! I'm a grown ass woman."

"Well, take your grown ass out of my house," he spat back.

I tried to hold back my laughter. But this whole argument was so funny, I couldn't help myself. However, I tried snickering very quietly. Unfortunately, it wasn't quite enough, because Ms. Kim heard me. "So, you think this shit is funny, huh?"

"I wasn't laughing at you," I lied, trying to prevent another argument from happening. I was really not in the mood. So I hoped she'd cut me some slack.

"Well, who the fuck was you laughing at?" she asked sarcastically, and then she took two steps towards me.

Devin must've thought something was about to go down because he interfered really quick.

"Kim, carry your stupid ass home right now," he demanded.

"Fuck that! I was here first. And now you're going to let this dirty looking bitch come up in here like she's better than me. Nah, this shit ain't happening!"

"Bitch! Who the fuck you calling dirty?" I roared. At this point, I was fed up with her blatant disrespect. Okay, granted, I looked a hot mess but she could've checked that dirty comment to herself. I had no intentions of breaking up there little nightcap. All I wanted was a place to lay my head tonight and then I was going to be out in the morning. But no, she gotta get all personal like she wanna run up on me. She better check herself before I take her motherfucking head off her shoulders.

"I'm talking to you, dirty girl!" she replied, and then she took two more steps towards me.

Now I wasn't in the mood to beat this bitch down, but

I swear, if she acted like she wanted to take one swing at me, then I was going to beat her ass like she stole something. As a matter of fact, I was going to take out all my anger and frustrations on this bitch for everything I had been through in these last twelve hours. So if she knew what I knew she would get the fuck away from me as quickly as she could.

Luckily for her, Devin grabbed her by the arm and escorted her dumb ass out of the front door. She didn't go willingly. She made him put her ass out with force. She was kicking and screaming like crazy. "Get the fuck off me!" she started punching him in the back after he threw her over his shoulders.

I stood there and watched him struggle to get her out of the apartment. I had to admit that she was giving him a run for his money. Devin was an average height of a man but his frame was small. He had to be every bit of a hundred and forty pounds. And this chick, Kim, was at least a hundred and sixty pounds, but she was built up in all the right places.

After struggling for a mere two minutes, he finally got her out of his apartment. And once he was able to close and lock the front door, Kim went on a rampage by kicking and punching the front door. I stood there and watched Devin. He didn't know what to do. I thought at one point he was going to open the front door and snatch her ass back in here. But that's not what happened. He yelled through the door and told her if she didn't leave he would call the police. She, in turn, threatened that if he called the police, then she would tell that he had drugs in the house.

When I heard that, I was about to flip out. I wasn't about to get caught up in that bullshit. I had just gotten out of jail, so you know I wasn't trying to go back, especially behind a nigga's drugs that I wasn't fucking. Oh, hell no! I can't have that. So while she was outside his front door making an ass out of herself and screaming out loud how she was going to call the police herself and tell them he had drugs in his house, I got freaked out.

"Call 'em, bitch! I don't give a fuck! Now carry your fishy pussy ass home!" he yelled back through the front door.

I pulled on his shirt and said, "You don't have drugs in here do you?"

"I got some personal shit that I'm smoking, but that's it," he told me.

"Are you sure?" I pressed the issue. I had to know the truth. Yes, I was in his domain, and I needed a place to stay for the night, but I didn't need to put my freedom on the line for it. I would rather sleep on a bench in the park than to go back to jail for another crime I didn't commit. No way.

"Don't believe that bullshit she's saying. Just ignore her and go in the bathroom so you can change," he instructed me. So I took him for his word and left the room. When I got into the bathroom I could still hear Kim yelling from outside of the house. She was going off on Devin like some shit was about to pop off. That chick caused so much commotion that it wouldn't surprise me if the police came. And in order to block all that drama out, I decided to hop in the shower. I needed to whine down and get my mind right before I headed back out

CHEAPER *to* KEEP HER 2

into the streets tomorrow.

I wondered if the hot water would wash away and cleanse the sins of men.

LATER THAT NIGHT

*I*f I didn't have drama in my life, I wouldn't have anything.

By the time I got out of the shower, all the chaos had
come to a halt. I was so happy because it had gotten so
peaceful. I threw my wet clothes across the back of Devin's kitchen chair so they could dry completely and then
I grabbed a sheet from his hall closet. When I was about
to lay down on this living room sofa, he scared the shit
out of me when he opened up the front door and walked
back into the apartment.

"I didn't know you were outside. I thought you were
in your bedroom," I said and then I took a seat on the sofa.

Devin flopped down on the couch beside me. "I had
to go outside and calm her silly ass down. She wasn't
gonna leave unless I talked to her," he told me. He tried
to act like he had really done something spectacular. I
listened to the mess he was trying to fill my head up with

and acted like I was extremely sorry for everything that went on. But I honestly didn't give a fuck. I was dry and I was about to get me some much needed rest, so I could care less.

"Where is she now?" I asked.

"She got in her car and went home."

I smiled. "Just like that?" I asked jokingly.

Devin smiled back. "Nah, not really. I had to tell her some shit she wanted to hear and then she left."

"Come on, Devin, stop bullshitting me. It took more than just that. I mean, I know she wanted to know who I was."

He looked at me bashfully. I knew that look. He used to give it to me when I caught his ass in a lie. "Yeah, she wanted to know how I knew you and if I ever fucked you."

"What did you tell her?"

"I told her nah."

"Nah, what?"

"I told her no me and you ain't never fucked and that you were like my baby sister."

"And she bought that lame ass story?"

"She's gone, ain't she?"

I smacked him against his arm. "You still ain't shit!"

"Ouch!" he said, covering up his arm with his other hand.

"Oh boy, shut up! That little smack didn't hurt," I told him and then I laid my head back against the headrest.

"You're tired, ain't you?"

I yarned. "Yes, I am exhausted. I've been running all day long it seems like," I began to say and then I paused.

UNIQUE

"Why you stopped talking?" he wanted to know.

"I was finished," I lied.

He looked at me strange because he knew when I was lying. And now, it seemed more obvious than in the past. Granted, we had history, but I knew Devin never really took me seriously, so he never had my best interest at heart. He was one of those typical niggas who wanted a woman in his life when it was convenient for him. He figured that when feelings got involved, shit got complicated. So I kept my mouth shut. Telling him everything I had been through wouldn't mattered to him . . . because he wouldn't have done shit about it.

"Well, at least tell me how the hell you got your clothes wet like that? You looked like somebody threw your ass in a pool."

"That's exactly what happened," I lied once again.

"Really!"

"Yep," I replied nonchalantly.

"So, whose house were you at?"

"I was at a hotel with a couple people I knew. And after that stupid shit happened, I left."

"When did you get out of jail?"

"Early this morning."

"Whatcha' out on bail?"

"Nah, the prosecutor dropped the charges because they didn't have enough evidence to convict me."

"Yo', let me tell you that when I heard about that shit I couldn't believe it. I was like, hell nah, Lynise ain't did no shit like that. But when I ran up on your home girl, Diamond, at the club about a few days after you got locked up, she was saying that you were wrapped up in a lot of shit. So I didn't know who or what to believe."

"Fuck that bitch! She was the one that help that motherfucker set me up. But it's cool. She'll get hers!" I snapped.

Devin threw his hands up. "Hold up! Don't kill the messenger."

"I'm just saying that what she did was really fucked up. She let a piece of dick come between us. Plus, she lied on me. So I will never forgive her for that shit!"

"You said the same shit about me."

"What?"

"That you'll never forgive me."

"I haven't," I replied sarcastically and then I smiled.

Devin reached over and tickled me in my side. "So, why you here?"

I giggled because he was tickling me in my weak spots. I tried to push his hands away from me, but he was just a little stronger than I was. "You better answer me," he pressed the issue.

"If you let me go then I can answer you," I continued to force him away from me.

He tickled me a couple more times and then he left me alone. After I got myself together, I looked at him and told him the truth without making myself look any worse than I'd already had. It was simple. I wasn't cool with any of my family and after Diamond had stabbed me in the back, I was no longer a part of her world. And even though Devin had hurt me time and time again behind his infidelities, I still had mad love for him . . . which reminded me that I needed to keep my pussy to myself tonight.

UNIQUE

Devin and I got along better before we started fuck-ing. And not that it mattered anyway, considering he'd just gotten him some pussy before I got here. "Look, De-vin, I would love to talk to you until the sun comes up, but I am extremely tired, so please let me get at least a couple hours of sleep."

He took another long look at me and then he said, "Okay. A'ight. I'll let you get some sleep." Before he got up from the sofa, he pat me on my thigh, "If you want to come and get in the bed with me, then you know where I am."

"Yeah, okay," I said and then I went into a zone. I heard him when he walked down the hallway and entered his room. I assumed he'd close his door but he didn't. He probably figured I'd get desperate enough and try to come and get in the bed with him. He was definitely irre-sistible but I had enough of his bullshit. And after what went down tonight with Ms. Kim, it would be in my best interest to let her have Devin and all the fucking drama that came with him.

I tossed and turned all night and couldn't get one wink of sleep from thinking about the shit that happened at Katrina's house. I even thought about where I would've been if I hadn't jumped off the ledge of her house. Who knows, I'd probably be dead somewhere stuffed inside of a couple of garbage bags. Or even worse, I could've been getting tortured and dying a slow and painful death right now. Boy, what a tragedy that would be. And the messed up part about it is that the little bit of family I had wouldn't even give a fuck. Not once while I was locked up did I get a fucking card or a visit from any of them. The thought of me being related to them made me sick to my stomach and from this day forward, I promised myself that I was going to deal with this situation I've gotten myself into and then I was going to get out of this God-forsaken place. And if it meant that I wouldn't see any one of them again, then so be it.

After tossing and turning half of the night, I finally dozed off. I woke up around nine in the morning and went straight to the bathroom. When I walked inside, I found Devin sitting on the toilet taking a shit. The fact I walked in on him while he was indisposed and the smell from his shit caught me off guard. I backed out of the bathroom immediately after I went in. "I'm sorry, I didn't know you were in here," I apologized.

"You all right," he assured me.

But in all actuality, I wasn't all right. I had just inhaled a ton of his shit, and then on top of that, I witnessed him getting on the toilet with his pants down. So how was I going to come back from that one?

"Can you please hurry up?" I yelled through the door.

"Go in my room and use the other bathroom."

"Okay," I said.

"Wait, go in the kitchen and get you a couple sheets of paper towels because I ran out of toilet paper in the bathroom."

I sighed heavily as I did as he instructed me to do.

Once I had a few sheets of paper towels in hand I raced through Devin's bedroom to the master bathroom. I quickly inspected the toilet seat before I sat down. I couldn't imagine sitting down on a toilet seat with dried piss spots on it. That would definitely send me over the edge. The thought of it alone made my skin crawl. So I immediately copped a squat and handled my business.

I was in and out of his bathroom in less than two minutes flat. When I exited his bedroom he was coming out of the other bathroom and we met in the hallway. He had a newspaper tucked away underneath his armpits. His face showed a sign of relief and he looked like he was five pounds lighter. He displayed all the traditional signs of taking a shit. I smiled and told him that he looked like he dropped a few pounds.

He smiled back at me. "Oh, so you got jokes now?"

I walked by him and headed back into the living room. "Nope."

He followed me momentarily and made a detour into the kitchen. I heard him drop the newspaper on the table and then I heard the refrigerator door open. "I'm about to eat a bowl of cereal. Do you want some?"

"Nah, I'm cool."

He peeped his head around the corner. I saw him through my peripheral vision.

"You sure?"

I turned towards him and said, "Yes, I am sure."

"A'ight now, don't be salivating all over my Fruity Peebles when I start eating them."

"Oh trust me, I won't."

While Devin fixed himself a bowl of cereal, I grabbed the remote-control and hit the power button. I kind of figured nothing was worth watching on TV besides the news. I was tired of dead bodies and sad ass news and truthfully, I wasn't ready to hear about somebody else's body being found. So I surfed through the channels and decided to watch a little bit of SpongeBob. I loved this cartoon just like all of the other kids. Plus, SpongeBob kept me from the reality that was going on around me. I didn't want to think about what was going on outside of Devin's front door, so I turned the volume up and lost myself in the show.

It shocked me to have Devin come and take a seat next to me. It seemed like he enjoyed the cartoon more than me. We both sat there and laughed until we couldn't laugh anymore.

In my mind, I wonder why life couldn't be this simple and enjoyable all the time.

UNIQUE

Playing with Fire

D evin's *Blackberry started ringing off the hook while we were watching TV.*
I thought it was reality shaking me back to the here and now. SpongeBob was my temporary escape.

For a moment, I thought it was that ghetto chick, Kim, but when Devin answered the phone and said, "What's good nigga?," I figured it out that it wasn't Kim. I couldn't hear the caller but the farther Devin got into the call, I figured out what they were talking about.

"Get the fuck out of here. Nigga, say it ain't so!" Devin said as he looked at me.

I looked back at him and hunched my shoulders as if to say, why you looking at me? He didn't response to my gesture but he did continue on with his conversation.

"So when did this shit happen?" He paused why the other person talked. "Man, please tell me you bullshitting me!" he begged and fell silent again. "Do you know I almost went up in there last night? If Kim wouldn't had called me last night and asked me if she could come over here, I would've been up in that spot last night." He paused again so the other caller could get a word in.

"Yo' man, I owe Kim my life. I mean, do you know I would probably be a dead motherfucker if she didn't want to give me some pussy last night?" he said and then he stood up from the chair. I watched him leave the living room as he continued his conversation. I could tell the thought of him getting killed while he was getting a lap dance inside of Magic City wore heavy on his mind, which was why he had to get up and walk around his apartment.

But you know what? He was right. He probably would've been inside of the club last night when it blew up. He was known to make it rain in there with his one dollar bills. That's where I met his no-good ass! Magic City was his spot. He loved that place like he loved pussy. For him not to be in there the night that it caught on fire spoke volumes. If he knew like I knew, he'd better be thanking the Good Lord above instead of Kim's dumb ass.

He re-entered the living room immediately after he got off the phone. I pretended like I was engrossed in what was going on in TV land. "Yo' home boy, Neil, just told me that somebody blew up Magic City last night while people were in there."

I acted like I was surprised. I didn't want Devin to know I knew anything about the explosion. I didn't want to be associated with it at all. "Nah, I didn't know that," I replied.

I didn't want to seem coldhearted. That would've

UNIQUE

been a dead giveaway. Devin would've either suspected I knew who did it or I was involved in it somehow. I was sure he heard rumors that I had gotten blackballed around town. After all the shit that went down with Duke, he made sure I couldn't get a job bartending in any of the clubs in the Tidewater area. So I had to play my cards very carefully with this guy. He didn't give a fuck about anyone but himself.

When we dated, I was just another piece of pussy he could run up in. I didn't mean shit to him. And I knew I really didn't mean a thing to him now, especially since he wasn't bending me over. He wasn't loyal to me when we were fucking, so I knew he wouldn't be loyal to me in the streets. So whatever secrets I had I knew I would be safer if I kept everything under close watch.

He shook his head and sat down next to me. He looked as if he had just lost his best friend or something. I had to know what was on his mind, so I asked him what was he thinking about.

He sat in a daze and then said, "I can't believe people were in that joint last night when that shit blew up. People I knew, people I had talked to, chicks who gave me lap dances."

"What time it happened?" I asked.

"Neil said the news people said it happened around seven or eight o'clock last night. He said he heard it was packed in there. And that a few niggas he knew said that they had just left before it happened."

"Wow! That's scary," I commented.

Devin continued to shake his head. And then he turned around and faced me, "Do you know that one of those dead bodies could've been mine? I would be dead right now if Kim didn't call me and asked me if she could come by here last night."

"I realize that," I replied.

He took his focus off me and picked up the remote control. I sat back and watched him surf through at least twenty channels until he got to Channel 10.

He waited for a broadcast to feature the story on Magic City, but nothing appeared in the thirty minutes while we sat around and watched. I had the urge to tell him I was there and I saw everything. I even wanted to tell him that Neeko's brother got killed while I was waiting for him inside his truck. But again, I knew it would've been a bad idea.

Devin wasn't someone I could trust. I've known him to gossip more than a bitch. And for him to come back in the room and tell me all of what his friend, Neil, told him, I knew he'd get right back on the phone and call Neil up and tell him everything I told him. And then from there, Neil would be calling niggas he knew and before I knew it, I'd be the talk of the fucking town. And I didn't need that type of attention. It was bad enough that I was trying to keep Duke and Chris off my ass.

So I figured I'd be in good shape if I didn't let this big mouth ass nigga know what I knew.

Moments later, he got another call. This time it was Kim. She must've said something about what happened at Magic City last night, because he got up from the couch and said, "I know. I just heard about it from my boy Neil." Then he left the room again. He didn't go that far because I can hear every word of this conversation.

UNIQUE

The first part of the conversation made me sick to my stomach. He kept telling her over and over again how grateful he was that she called him last night and prevented him from going to the club. As much as I wanted to believe him, I knew what he was saying was bullshit. Yeah, he was grateful today, but he'll be calling her a bitch tomorrow. That's just how he rolled.

After several minutes of kissing her ass, he fed her some bullshit ass lie about how he thought he was ready to settle down. He told her he also believed the only reason why God used her to prevent him from going out last night was so that he could have a chance to get his life together.

I swear, if I had a violin I would have serenaded that whack ass conversation he was having with her. With all the shit he had done in his life, it was gonna take him two lifetimes to make up for it. So the only reason why I believed God spared his life was so he could find something for recreational to do other than exploit naked ass women with those measly ass dollar bills he fed them. In other words, God gave that bastard another chance because he felt sorry for his silly ass! That's it! *End of Story.*

Devin's bullshit lies lasted approximately five minutes. But before he hung up with the dumb ass chick, he lied to her once more and told her I had left his apartment before he got up. I mean, if she believed that then she was sillier than I gave her credit for. And to add insult to injury, he even told her that he loved her. I swear, I almost laughed out loud and blew his cover.

When he came back in the living room, I smiled at him and said, "So, you're in love, huh?"

He smiled. "I might be," he said and then he sat back down on the couch next to me. "I wonder if your girl, Diamond, was in the club when it blew up."

I hunched my shoulders as if I couldn't care less. I knew she wasn't there, but I wasn't going to let him know it. "If she was, it served her right," I commented, then I rolled my eyes. The sound of her name made me cringe all over.

"Damn, that's kind of fucked up to say."

"It ain't no more fucked up than how she carried me!" I snapped. "Me and her were like two peas in the pod. We did everything fucking thing together. We were inseparable. When she didn't have, I had it for her. So for her to double cross me like she did was foul. I swear, I would spit on that bitch's grave if I had the opportunity."

Devin started rubbing my back in a circular motion. I figured this was his way of telling me that everything would be all right. Whether he knew it or not, once upon of time I would've spit on his fucking grave too, especially with all the drama he caused me during our courtship. He better be glad he let me into this apartment last night, because I was on the verge of fucking up his car if he hadn't.

Devin allowed me to vent a little bit more and then he flipped the script on me and asked me what did I have planned today? I had to admit that he kind of caught me off guard with that question because I really didn't know where I was going. I thought I would've come up with a plan overnight but it didn't happen, so what was I going to do? I looked at Devin in hopes that he'd help me come up with an answer. But he was just as clueless as I was.

UNIQUE

"I was planning on calling my sister, Nita, when I think she's off work," I finally said. But it was an outright lie. I believed he knew it too.

"I didn't know that you and your sister, Nita, were back speaking again," he commented.

"We just started back talking before I got out," I continued to lie. I did this because if I let on that I had no one in my corner, then he'd use that shit against me. He'd love to know that I needed him. He'd eat that shit up for breakfast, lunch and dinner. Especially after all the times I dissed him at the club. He'd relish in the moment if he knew I had nowhere to go. And he'd try to milk it for what it's worth.

"How your mama doing?" he surprised me again. But I knew what he was doing. Devin and I dated for over a year, so he knew I didn't fuck with none of my family. That included my mama's money hungry ass too. So he either asked me that question to be nosey or he just wanted to make idle conversation.

"I haven't spoken to her. But Nita said she was fine," my lies kept coming.

"Do you think she found out about you copping that murder charge?"

"I'm sure she did. But Nita didn't say anything about it," I replied.

When Devin was about to ask me another one of his dumb ass questions, his doorbell rang. He looked at me very strange. "I wonder who that is?" he said aloud as he got up from the sofa.

I got up from the sofa as well, but I headed into the bathroom, because I needed to empty my bladder. Right after I closed the door to the bathroom and locked it, I heard Devin yell out, "Who is it?"

I didn't hear anything else because the sound of me peeing overpowered what was being said in the other room. So I handled my business and allowed Devin to handle his.

And I wondered if kings of old ever made any big decisions while they sat on the toilet.

UNEXPECTED GUEST

*E*ven fortunes of the stupid have to change some-
times.

I flushed the toilet, washed my hands and exited
the bathroom. But as soon as I re-entered the living room,
Devin wasn't anywhere to be found. I called his name out
twice, but I still got no answer. So I walked to the front
door and noticed it was cracked, so I grabbed a hold of
the doorknob and pulled it open. I looked outside but he
was still nowhere in sight. It really seemed weird that
he'd leave his fucking front door cracked and then he disappeared. *I mean, who in the hell does that?*

I didn't know whether to close the door and lock it or
go outside to see where the hell he went. But then it
dawned on me that maybe Duke and Chris found out
where I was and grabbed Devin up so he wouldn't be in
the way when they killed me. The thought of them being
able to move on me like that gave me an eerie feeling. I
wasted no time locking the door, and then I rushed into

the kitchen to grab the sharpest knife Devin had. It seemed like everything I picked up was dull or rusty so I left them where they were.

Then I remembered Devin had a .45 caliber handgun he used to tuck away underneath his white tees in the bottom left drawer, so I rushed into his bedroom to see if it was still there. With my heart beating a mile a second, I ransacked his tee-shirt drawer and found it. After I picked up that heavy piece of metal I let out a long sigh of relief, because I knew if what I believed was true, then I would be able to fight those bastards off me with no problems.

Once I put it in my head which angle I was going to go at those niggas, I laid the gun down on the floor next to me and proceeded to place all of Devin's t-shirts back where they were. I knew Devin didn't check his tee-shirt drawer every day.

After that was done, I got up from the floor with Devin's gun in my right hand and I headed back down the hallway towards the living room. I honestly didn't know whether to sit back down on the sofa or hide in a fucking closet somewhere. I really didn't know what to do, so I decided to stand next to the front door and occasionally look through the peep hole.

Five minutes went by and I heard nothing and no one came to the door. Then all of a sudden, I heard footsteps and just as fast as I heard them, they stopped. My heart seemed like it stopped too. I held my breath to prevent anyone from hearing me. I wanted to look through the peephole but I got cold feet. Although the person on the outside couldn't see me, my eye against the peephole would prevent the reflected light from the inside of the house from appearing through the peephole, and whoever was on the other side of the door would know someone was inside.

Seconds later, someone turned the doorknob and tried to push on the door. "Lynise, open the door," I heard a guy yell. But it wasn't Devin. So my heart sunk into the pit of my stomach. I didn't know what the fuck to do. I knew I had Devin's pistol, so if this man on the other side tried to break down the fucking door, then I'd have some hot lead for his ass.

Whoever it was knocked a couple more times. "Lynise, are you in there?" the guy yelled through the door. But I didn't budge. For the life of me, I couldn't figure out who the fuck this man was standing outside Devin's front door. It didn't sound like Duke or Chris, so who in the hell was it? This shit wasn't cool. I didn't like this feeling.

I couldn't take it anymore. I had to risk being detected so I looked through the peephole and saw who this unidentified man was. I raced away from the door and then I yelled, "I'm coming," after I realized it was Devin's friend, Neil. Neil was his sidekick. So if he saw me with Devin's pistol in my hand, he wasn't going to receive it very well.

I rushed back down the hallway and shoved Devin's gun right back where I got it from and then I raced back down the hallway to open the front door. When Neil walked in, he looked at me pretty strange. "You all right?" he asked as he walked in slowly.

"Yeah, I'm cool," I lied.

"You sure?" he said.

CHEAPER *to* KEEP HER 2

"Yeah, I'm sure," I replied sarcastically.

"Well, why you sweating and shit?" he asked jokingly. Neil was a very handsome guy with excellent taste in
clothing, but he was also a fucking wise guy. So, I never
liked him. He had a huge influence on Devin's decision
making. When Devin and I were dating and I wanted him
to hang out with me, Neil would always come up with
some bullshit about how they had already made fucking
plans. That shit used to burn me up. Not only that, whenever Devin and I got into fights, Neil always threw in his
two cents. Truth be told, he was one of the main reasons
why Devin and I broke up. I thought he was Devin's un-
dercover lover at one point, so I used to tease him about
it. I knew he hated my fucking guts. But guess what? I
hated his fucking guts too, so we were even.

"Why the fuck are you always up in my space?" I responded.

Neil walked away from the door and headed towards
the kitchen. "Trust me, I'm not in your space," he replied
with his back facing me.

I ignored his immaturity and switched the conversation around. "Do you know where Devin is?" I asked
him.

He walked back into the living room with a beer in
his hand. "He's outside talking to some chick named Kim.
He's keeping her from coming in here and seeing you, so
you won't get your ass kicked!" he replied and then
smiled.

"You got your own opinions, and I got mines. And so
you know, she was already here when I broke up their
little rendezvous. So if she wanted to have a boxing

match with me, she would have tried her hand last night. End of story," I told him as I rolled my eyes.

He took a sip of his beer and said, "So you're proud that you got my homeboy to pull his dick out of her pussy just so he could push it up in you?"

"Fuck you, Neil! For your information, I didn't fuck Devin last night. I'm not skanky like those hoes you fuck with. I've got more class than any woman you ever been with. So get a grip on yourself! You're looking really tacky right now sipping on a beer at ten-thirty in the morning. That's a sure sign of a broke ass alcoholic!"

Neil took another sip of his beer and then he smiled. "Is this your way of venting your frustrations because your life is pretty much fucked up right now? And in order for you to feel good about yourself, you try to find fault in other people."

"Neil, please shut the fuck up! You don't know shit about my life. So stay in your own lane please."

Neil was about to come back at me with another one of his sarcastic remarks, but Devin stopped all of the bullshit when he walked through the door. "Yo'! Yo'! Yo'! I can hear y'all when I was walking up the stairs," he commented.

I sucked my teeth. "If your best friend would mind his own business, then the world and everybody in it would be better off," my sarcasm continued.

"Come on now, let's not fight, boys and girls," he said with humor as he closed the door and took a seat on the sofa. He looked directly at Neil and said, "Yo', dude, did you see how she was acting?"

Neil sat down in the recliner across from Devin.

"Yeah, I saw her. She's gonna be unmanageable if you don't get her ass straight now."

"I know. I'm gonna probably have to break up with her ass sooner than I thought," Devin told Neil.

I wanted to shake my head and ask Devin did he remember last night when he was talking marriage and shit because he thought Kim had saved his life. Short term memory. That was the shit too many of us suffered with.

And to hear these two talking about this chick really rubbed me the wrong way. Okay, granted, I didn't exactly like her ass after she made that comment about how dirty I looked. Hell, I would have kicked Duke's and a bitch's ass for barging in on us in the wee hours of the morning. But still, it made me sick to my stomach that Neil had so much influence on Devin. I mean, mind your own business. Get your own girlfriend, you fucking loser!

In the middle of their back and forth conversation about Devin's new play toy, Kim, I interjected and asked Devin if he minded if I went into his room and laid down on his bed. He told me he didn't mind, so I got up and left.

While Neil continued to give jackass relationship advice, Devin's Blackberry rang. He left it on top of his dresser, so I got off the bed, grabbed it and took it to him. But by the time I handed it to him, it had stopped ringing. He took it from me and then I returned back to his bedroom and climbed back onto his bed. I'm sure he knew I looked down at the screen to see who was calling. He didn't mention it though. I laid there in silence and waited for him to call Ms. Olivia back. I shook my head as I wondered how men, but him in particular, could fuck

two and three bitches at one time. It just angered me that
he could never be faithful.

While Kim had questioned him about me, she needed
to be worried about all the other bitches he was creeping
with. *Niggas will never change!*

I dosed off for about an hour but Devin woke me up
to tell me he had to make a run with Neil. "Don't go
snooping through my shit!" he warned me.

"You ain't gotta worry about that," I assured him.
And I meant that from the bottom of my heart. I will admit that I used to go through his shit but it was only because we were dating. Believe me, he gave me many reasons to search his pants pockets and look through his text
messages to see what new bitch he was fucking behind
my back. But now, I wouldn't waste my time. He's
shown me at least five times within the last ten hours that
he had not changed and he had no intentions of doing so.

I did however search his bottom drawer to see if he'd
taken his gun with him. But he didn't. I was relieved to
know that if any funny business went down, then I'd be
okay after I pumped a couple of rounds of those lead pellets in a nigga's ass.

*It's crazy how guns and knives give muthafuckas false
bravado.*

Zero Ways to Communicate

S leep is for the weary—the way to success is to wake up, get up and get moving.

I slept for about another hour and then I became restless, so I got up. Devin's apartment was completely quiet. I could hear a pin drop if I had one to throw on the floor. Since I didn't, I headed into the kitchen to see what he had in the refrigerator to eat. I was so hungry I could feel my stomach in my back. Unfortunately for me, he didn't have a damn thing to eat. The box of cereal he had was empty, but he had plenty of milk left. I noticed that he had a cartoon of eggs too, but when I grabbed it, the motherfucking thing was empty. I mean, who does that dumb shit? If we were still dating I would be furious with his selfish ass right now. So I made do by getting a large glass of milk and then I stuck four slices of bread into the toaster oven and when they were done, I spread some butter on them and topped it off with a couple packages of strawberry preserve I found in his kitchen drawer. It

UNIQUE

wasn't an International House of Pancakes meal, but it served its purpose.

As soon as I started to enjoy my quiet time, I heard some chick fussing outside of Devin's front door. It became apparent she was gossiping with her home girl on her cell phone, because I didn't hear anyone else's mouth but hers. After my so-called breakfast, I took a sit in the living room so I could watch a little bit of TV. But then it dawned on me that she'd probably let me use her cell phone if I asked nicely. I immediately got up from the sofa and opened the front door. I realized I scared her because she jumped as soon as she saw me.

"I am so sorry if I scared you," I told her with a smile on my face.

She smiled in return. "No, it's okay. I'm probably talking to loud, huh?" she asked me. I wanted to tell her what I really thought but I didn't. I figured it would lessen my chances of getting her to agree to let me use her phone. Not only that, she was a big, heavyweight Amazon chick. She had to be every bit of six feet and weighing about three hundred pounds. And like true Amazon women, it was packed tight and solid on her body. I didn't think the average nigga would run up on her. Aside from how huge she was, she was kind of cute and she seemed like a sweetheart.

"Nah, you're fine," I lied. "But I do want to know if I could use your phone when you're done. 'Cause, see, the guy who lives here doesn't have a home phone and since I left my cell phone at my best friend's house, I was trying to get in touch with her to see if I could get her to drop it off to me," Which was also a lie.

CHEAPER *to* KEEP HER 2

"Oh yeah, that'll be no problem," she said in a naturally loud voice. I couldn't see her trying to sneak and whisper to anyone. She placed the phone back to her mouth, "Janet, let me call you back in like five minutes. I'm gonna let this lady use my phone."

Immediately after she ended her call, she gave me her cell. I thanked her after I took the phone from her hand.

"Knock on my door when you're finished," she instructed me as she turned around and went into her apartment, which was directly across from Devin's place.

I looked down at the keypad of Devin's neighbor's cell phone and had no idea who I was going to call. My mind drew a complete blank. "Come on, Lynise, there's gotta be somebody you can call," I mumbled to myself. And then it dawned on me that I had taken down Rodney's cell phone number while I was watching Diamonds apartment.

I rushed back into Devin's apartment, leaving the front door open to retrieve Rodney's number from my pants pocket. But when I dug inside all my pockets, I couldn't find it. Damn, I was pissed at myself.

I started to take Devin's neighbor her phone back when I noticed Devin had left his car keys on the coffee table in the living room. I came up with the perfect idea. I knew if he allowed me to use his car for a couple of hours, then I would be able to make a few moves. Going to talk to those two homicide detectives was one-stop I had to make, since I no longer had Bishop around to help me sort things out.

When I dialed his number I knew he wasn't going to answer but it didn't matter because I was going to leave him a message anyway. Needless to say, he did the unexpected and answered the call on the second ring. I was shocked.

"Yo', what's up, Kesha?" he said.

"This isn't Kesha. It's Lynise," I told him.

"What's up?"

"I was calling to ask you if I could use your car for about an hour or so."

"Where you going?"

"I wanna run by my sister's job and then I wanna go to the store to pick up a few things," I lied. I knew I couldn't tell him the real reason why I wanted to use his car. He would've told me no with the quickness.

"Yeah, go ahead but you better not have a nigga riding around in my shit with you."

"Devin, no one does that trifling shit but you," I assured him.

"I don't do that shit either," he expressed. But I quickly cut him short by telling him thank you and that I would be putting gas in his car when I was done with it.

"Have it there when I get back," he instructed.

"What time is that?"

"I'll probably be back around four o'clock."

I looked at the time on his neighbor's cell phone and noticed I had three hours to play with, so I promised him I would have it back by that time.

"Lock my door. And don't try to make a spare key while you're out," he yelled through the phone.

"All right," was the last thing I said before ending the call.

CHEAPER *to* KEEP HER 2

I knocked on Kesha's door and returned her cell phone as soon as I got off the phone with Devin. I thanked her about three times before she could close her front door. "No problem, anytime," she said before we parted ways.

Back inside of Devin's apartment, I put back on the clothes I had on yesterday since they were completely dry. I made my exit from the apartment and jumped in Devin's whip, a black, two-door Nissan 350Z with smoked gray tinted windows. This car was his prize possession, so it shocked me when he gave me permission to drive. When we dated, I can remember only driving it three times. It sat really low to the ground, so I had to hunch down to climb inside. There wasn't a lot of room inside of the car either. But I wasn't going to let that deter me because all I needed was for this vehicle to take me from point A to point B. And that was it.

Immediately after I turned on the ignition and revved up the engine, I put the little remote control car in gear and headed towards the highway. I was really nervous about the idea, but I decided to ride by Katrina's house. I had to see if Duke's car was still there or not. I wanted to see if Bishop's truck was still parked there as well as see if there was any sign of Katrina. If her car was there and Duke's wasn't, that may be a good sign. However, that could also be a trap. What if Duke or Chris was hiding in the house, waiting on my stupid ass to return? Then again, who knows, Duke may had both of Katrina's and Bishop's vehicles towed away from the house, so the police wouldn't link the tags to Bishop.

My heart raced at a rapid speed while my mind thought of the many ways I could get caught by driving back to Katrina's house. It was clear that I was treading on dangerous waters, but I knew of no other way to handle this. Maybe I was a glutton for punishment.

It only took me twenty minutes to drive from Devin's apartment to Katrina's gated community. To get to her house was like traveling through a maze but I managed. And as soon as I made a left turn onto her street I noticed that Bishop's truck was still parked in front of the house, but Katrina's Audi and Duke's Porsche were gone.

I wanted to exhale but I couldn't when I saw the entire front part of the house was taped off with yellow homicide tape. CRIME SCENE – DO NOT CROSS. The black letters on yellow background stood out. My heart sunk deep into the pit of my stomach as my eyes and mouth widened. I couldn't fucking believe what I was seeing.

A part of me wanted to stop at one of the neighbor's houses to ask them what went on. But I knew it wouldn't be a good idea. So I continued to cruise by the house without stopping. Luckily for me, Devin's car windows were tinted to the point that no one could see inside, even if they got really close to the car. This was one good advantage I had. I just hoped and prayed no one was looking out the window and decided to write down Devin's license's plate numbers. That wouldn't be good at all. So I pressed down on the accelerator and rushed to get my ass out of this neighborhood.

His crazy ass had killed his meal ticket! I could only imagine what he would do to me.

My Eyes Playing Tricks on Me

Who said Christmas only comes once a year?

I was almost at the end of Katrina's street, approaching a stop sign, when the black Cadillac Escalade pulled in front of me and stopped my passage. Before I could I put the car in reverse, two niggas with guns jumped out of the passenger side doors and rushed towards the car. If I tried to get away, I knew I would be dead. My brain was telling me to gun it in reverse. The guns gave me second thoughts.

Neither one of them said a word. One was big, at least six foot four, mean looking. The other one was shorter, not six feet but close, with a slim build. He was the leader of the two. I could tell when he signaled me to get out of the car with his index finger. I so reluctantly complied.

I thought that maybe I could talk my way out of this situation. Maybe Duke would show some compassionate

UNIQUE

for what little relationship we did have. I prayed one of Katrina's neighbors was watching out the window and called the police. I also prayed that they would make it here before I was gunned down in the street.

When I stepped out of the car, the driver side door of the Escalade opened. It was on the other of the car, so I didn't see the driver when he initially got out the car. I was hoping I didn't pee in my pants when I saw Duke. As he walked around the car, it wasn't Duke at all.

It was Bishop and he increased his pace as he rounded the front of the car.

Suddenly my legs had life in them as I ran towards him. I don't know what had gotten in me when I jumped in his arms as if this was an old-fashioned black and white movie. But Bishop was definitely my black knight. I held him tight . . . and equally, I was happy to say he held me just as tight. His left arm held and caressed my back while his right hand was on the back of my head holding my head tight on his chest. At that moment, Bishop was my hero.

I don't know how long we stayed in that position. It could have been a minute or five minutes. I didn't know and frankly, I didn't give a damn. But reality has a way of fucking up golden moments.

"We probably need to get out of here," I said as I slowly removed my head from Bishop's chest.

"Whose car you driving?" he asked me.

"A friend."

He looked like he was surprised. "Didn't think you had any more friends?" he said in the form of a question than a statement.

CHEAPER *to* KEEP HER 2

"Not many," was my short answer.

He turned to his guys and circled his finger in the air and walked towards Devin's car. I stopped him. "Bishop, this car belongs to a male friend of mines. It would probably be disrespectful if I let another man ride in it," I said. "Can you just follow me?"

"No," was his one word answer.

What the fuck!

He grabbed my hand. Not in a rough way but definitely in a manly, take control way. He led me to the passenger side and opened the door for me. Then he went on the driver side and before you knew it, we were on the road with his henchmen in tow.

As we made our way to Devin's place, I had to know how he had escaped the club before it blew up. I didn't hesitate to bring the subject up. "Please tell me how the fuck you got out of the club. I just knew you were dead."

"When I went in and didn't see Katrina in the front area or around the bar, I went to the back, the office area," Bishop began telling me. "So when I didn't see her in the office area, I became leery and went out the back door, not expecting that the whole place was going to blow up. I thought she was going to have a nigga run up on me and put a bullet in the back of my head, since I was the only one in the back part of the club."

I couldn't respond to what he was saying because I was still in shock that he was alive after all this time.

"I'll tell you what, whoever planted that bomb knew what the hell they were doing because a lot of innocent people either died instantly or burned to death. Thank God I got out in the nick of time. But the explosion did knock me unconscious. Plus, some of the debris fell on me as well. I don't know how long I was out."

He paused and looked at me. He smiled and that one gesture told me all would be well. And I don't know why I did what I did next, which was I put my hand on his hand. He gave me a squeeze and shit, I damned near came in my pants.

"When I came to," Bishop started back talking, "the firemen were starting to check the debris in the back area where I was. I managed to sneak away without being detected. I got this chick to take me back to the hotel and immediately called a couple of my guys to come down and help me handle business. The girl at the hotel told me you had come by, got a key and had left back out, but never came back."

He looked at me again. Something told me he didn't need nor want an explanation. He flashed that smile again and I knew I was wet.

"After I got cleaned up, I checked into another hotel," Bishop continued. "I tried to get some rest but I couldn't. Getting that bitch Katrina wore heavy on my mind. So I sat up all night and waited on my boys to get here, which didn't take long since they were in D.C. The waiting gave me time to think about a lot of shit. And what I came up with was how I'm gonna make that grimy bitch wish she hadn't crossed me. All last night I couldn't get her off my mind. And the fact that I know she set me up made me believe that she had my brother, Neeko, set up too."

As I looked at Bishop, I saw his facial expression change as the veins in his neck and around the temple of his forehead started sticking up through his flesh. It was a combination of sadness, hurt, anger and danger. It was at that point that I realized I had misread him. He was indeed a dangerous man. The fact he was alive should have told me that. But the true sign was how he smelled trouble within a couple of minutes of being in the club, and smelling a set-up. In the 'hood they would say, "He's the muthafucka!" *And he was.*

"I know how badly you wanted to take Katrina out but it seems like Duke already beat you to the punch. You did see all that yellow tape wrapped around the front part of her house, didn't you?"

Bishop looked back at me and gave me this wicked ass smiled. "Oh no, he didn't," he commented. And at the moment it felt as if I was in the twilight zone. I instantly wondered how he was able to get to Katrina when Duke was with her. And when I couldn't put two and two together, I asked him.

"Immediately after my boys got here we went straight to her crib. We scoped it out before I snuck into the house from the back. She was in her bedroom . . . actually the master bathroom when I walked up on her. And when she saw me she was definitely surprised to see me. But I was more surprised to see how Duke had beaten the shit out of her. Her entire face was bruised up and the swelling sat out at least two inches from her face. Her eyes were blacked and he even knocked a couple of teeth out of her mouth. She looked really bad. "

Bishop's voice was deliberate and methodical. His tone was even. He was a man in control . . . in more ways than one. He was straight to the point. He didn't throw in adjectives or superlatives to impress me. He was just telling me what I needed to know. What I probably didn't want to hear.

Katrina in her own way had saved me. And even before he told me, I knew now that it was Bishop who killed Katrina. "I didn't hit her," Bishop pressed on with the story. "I told her to tell me everything and if she left out one thing or lied to me, I would kill her whole damn family, starting with the kids. So she told me everything. She even told me what she told you and how you were able to get away from Duke." He cracked another slight smile when he said that. But just as quickly his demeanor changed and his eyes grew dark again. He was a scary cat.

"After she told me what I needed to know, I let her know that her kids would be taken care of and the rest of her family would live to see another day."

And then he was quiet. We drove in quietness for at least another five minutes before I had to ask the question. "How did you kill her?" I had to ask. It damn near killed me not to know how he ended her life.

"I broke her fucking neck, called the police and reported the crime and described the person leaving her house as a man who looked like Duke Carrington," he said matter-of-factly.

The rest of the ride was driven in silence. Rest in peace, Katrina, I'm sorry but you picked the wrong team.

MASSIVE ATTACK

*W*ars are won in the strategy room, drawing up a
plan and creating chaos in the mind.

We arrived at Devin's apartment complex and
parked Devin's car back in his assigned parking space. I
prayed the whole way that Devin hadn't come back home
yet. Something awful would've jumped off if Devin saw
Bishop driving his car.

Neil would have punked Devin into sticking his chest
out and Bishop would have put him in the Intensive Care
Unit . . . or worse, killed him. I liked Devin and he had
finally come through for me. I didn't want to see him six
feet under. There were others who deserved that faith
way more than he did.

I placed Devin's car keys underneath the floor rug on
the driver side and then I locked both doors. Bishop and I
hopped in the back seat of the SUV. "Let's head back to
the hotel," he instructed the driver.

UNIQUE

On the way to the hotel, Bishop introduced me to the two cats he summoned here from D.C. The tallest one name was Torch and the shorter cat's name was Monty. Both had stoic expressions and looked like they were down for business—serious business. Monty looked like he didn't take any shit off anyone. He also looked like he could've been related to Bishop and Neeko. I started to ask him but I changed my mind.

Under circumstances like this, niggas didn't give up information about where they were from and who they knew. They weren't gonna tell me shit like who they fucked up, murdered or assassinated. Hell nah! Real niggas take care of their business and get the hell out of dodge without leaving any witnesses.

I realized Bishop and his two partners had gotten a hotel room at the Fairfield Inn on the corner of Military Highway and North Hampton Boulevard when we entered into the parking lot. Bishop told me he didn't usually stay in three-star hotels. It was all about four- or five-star hotels for him. This was a step down for him and his boys. I remembered how nice this hotel used to be when it was first built a few years back. Now it was considered a normal spot like the extended stay hotels.

"Let go," Bishop instructed me as soon as the truck came to a complete stop. I followed him to the room while Torch and Monty followed me. For some odd reason, I thought they had plans to get rid of my ass, but when Bishop and I went into his room and Torch and Monty went in the room next door, I let out a sigh of relief.

Once we were inside the room Bishop took a seat on the edge of the bed, while I sat in the chair at the small table. It was completely quiet but I knew he was about to say something. I could tell he was in deep thought, so I sat there and waited. And when he finally opened his mouth, I gave him my undivided attention.

"I'm impressed you made it out Katrina's house alive and well," Bishop said in a calm and soothing voice. I kinda smiled. I was somewhat speechless. This nigga really did impress me.

He really was a fucking black knight. He knew when to be a hardcore nigga, and when he needed to flip the script, he could be smooth as hell. His edges were polished as compared to Neeko's, who was still rough around the edges.

Hell, I had to admit I was attracted to hardcore, thuggish, ruggish ass niggas. But I wanted a man who could turn that shit off at the drop of a dime, and still be cool and smooth as silk. That's what I thought I had in Duke. But no, it was a fucking pretender.

Bishop was the real shit!

"We gotta figure out a way to smoke Duke out," he began. "I know where his ass lives and all of hideouts, but I know his ass won't be at any of those locations."

"How you know all of this shit and when I don't even know where that motherfucka lives? Hell, if I did, or even knew where he hangs his hat, I'd be the first to show you," I said.

Bishop smiled. "Even if you knew where he hung his hat when he isn't at home, he wouldn't be there because the police are probably looking for him as we speak."

"I don't think so. From the way Katrina laid it out to me, the two cats that Bishop owe money to got a few cops on payroll. So the police ain't gonna let nobody get close to that bastard until they get their money from him."

"Lynise, I want you to think on a large scale. Stop thinking on the basement level and think on the penthouse level. Yeah, these brothers have some cops and probably even city officials on their payroll, but in every city half the cops are on the take and the other half are straight as fucking arrows . . . the same with politicians. Men of power will never have complete control, because there is always someone more powerful with more control."

"I know the shit you are spitting out, Bishop, but this part of Virginia belongs to Duke and the two brothers," I said. Hell, he acted like I was dumb as shit.

"No, trust me on this Lynise," Bishop replied. "Those in the penthouse hope those in the basement believe men like Duke and the two brothers can do what they want. But it doesn't work that way. No, we have to smoke Duke and Chris out. One by one."

I didn't know what to say. He was adamant about what he was saying, and that shit was eloquent as hell. And I believed he knew what in the fuck he was talking about. After all, he was a millionaire I don't know how many times over and shit, beside the clothes on my back, I didn't have shit.

"Lynise, killing Katrina in her house was the key. If she was killed some other place, no one would have cared. But this was a nice neighborhood, a gated community. That in itself is already raising red flags at city hall and police headquarters. And that's what I wanted. I wanted Duke to go into hiding. Who know why?"

I quietly shook my head no, because I really didn't know his strategy. But he did. I could tell. And I was impressed. This muthafucka was genuine draft. He was the real shit.

"Because men like Duke don't know how to hide," he explained in perfect diction and that was fucking me up. As much as I wanted a hardcore, sophisticated nigga, I felt outclass, and no one had ever made me feel that way.

"He has to be seen," Bishop continued. "To be seen means his pure presence strikes fear in people. Those people on the basement level. That's what gives him his power. Now we have taken that power. But Duke can't survive without the power. He won't be underground long. But we still need something to smoke him out."

Fuck, I was motivated now. I wanted to help, to add something to the equation. And I could only think of one thing to help him accomplish his mission. Actually, I could think of one other person to help us get to Duke— that bitch, Diamond. She was the answer to our problem. Not only could we use her to lure Duke to us, we could also eliminate her ass in the process. Seeing that bitch squirm and beg for her life would be icing on the cake for me. What she did to me was unforgivable. And just like Katrina, she will also find out that she was on the wrong team.

"All we have to do is snatch that bitch Diamond up and her stupid ass will get Duke to come to us," I suggested.

"Did anyone move in with her after you got arrested?" *How in the hell did he know we were roommates?* "No, after I was arrested and her boyfriend got killed, she has lived by herself ever since."

"So she is in the same apartment you guys have had for a while?" What the fuck! "Ok, yes, she lives in the same apartment, in the same apartment building we have lived in for a while. But it would be easy to get to her because I got a little homeboy out her way that'll get her out of her apartment if need be."

"Nah, I don't want to lure her out of the apartment, I want to keep her inside and see if we can get Duke to come in there with her."

I shook my head immediately. "No, that's not going to work. Diamond lives in the hood. So when Duke's comes by he never steps foot out of his car."

"Do you know this for sure?"

"Yeah, I told you I got this young cat out there that sees everything. I talked to him last night and he told me that a few of his road dogs is waiting for the day that Duke steps foot out of his car so they can rob his ass and take his whip."

He didn't have a quick comeback. Once again he was in deep thought. Hell, so was I. How in the hell did this muthafucka know all of the information he knew. "Bishop, how you know we were roommates and where Duke lived and the other places he have?" I knew I took him out of his deep thoughts.

"Lynise, it's my business to know what I'm getting into and know about the people that affect my world." His words just hung in the air for a moment. "I know everything I need to know to make this work and then I can get my ass back home, away from this damn area."

I didn't know what to say. I didn't know where that would lead me after he reaped his revenge on Duke and Chris. Hell, I didn't even know if he was going after the two brothers or not. But he is obviously a man with resources and shit, I felt foolish for doubting him when we initially met.

"By the way, we might just be able to accommodate your friends," he replied. "I want to roll out of here as soon as it gets dark, so get yourself some rest and be ready by nightfall."

Sleep captured my heart, soul and body as soon as my head hit the pillow.

DEAD FRIENDS TELL NO TALES

Who knows how they will die—for many, it's still a guess a minute before their last breath.

The growling of my stomach woke me up and I knew Bishop was next door. I had only been sleeping a couple of hours. I knocked on the wall and within a minute he was there. I told him I was hungry. He asked what I wanted, and I told him Chinese. I watched him as he as he walked to the door. His body language and swagger were fucking me up inside. I supposed to be thinking about revenge on Diamond and Duke, and my mind was on Bishop's fine ass. I swear he was sexy as hell.

I still wondered how this whole thing would play out. And what was my destiny after we killed Duke. Would Bishop just leave and leave me here? I knew he had a bitch where he lived. I didn't know her, so I didn't give a damn about her. Something inside of me told me he deserved to be with a woman like me. But I knew I had tightened my shit up and become a little more sophisticated. In my heart I knew his ass was kicking with thugs and city officials—pimps and business suits. I just knew he rolled like that.

I really did have a thing for bad boys. I didn't know why. They just exuded power when I saw them handling their business in the streets. But Bishop was on another level. He was right about the penthouse and basement. He hobnobbed with both levels. Yeah, he was indeed a bad boy, but he had plenty of money to go with his power, and that shit was an added bonus and one helluva turn-on. I just knew his ass was invincible. And I was fucking love it. And what was even crazier was that I would still fuck him. Fuck his woman, I had to look out for me. Shit, I figured with everything going on and all the loyalty I had shown him, he would love to wife me up when all ended well. If not, fuck it, I would still give him a taste of this pussy.

When he made it back, I ate and was happy he ate with me. He let me go back to sleep and woke me up around eight that night and told me to get ready. If taking a shower and walking back in the room, I was surprised to see all of the clothes he had bought me. He just didn't know how I wanted to drop to my knees and stick his dick in my mouth. And then I hoped he would tongue fuck me like there was no tomorrow, before he slammed that dick in my wet pussy. And damn, I was some kind of wet.

UNIQUE

But that shit would have to wait. It didn't take me long to get dressed and ready. Now was the time for business. Pleasure had to wait for later.

When we got back into the SUV, initially, no one said a word. I didn't know if this was nervous energy or what. Maybe it was me. As we rolled out of the hotel, I was prepared to give Torch Diamond's address when Bishop told Monty the address and he put it in the GPS. Shit, this muthafucka knew the address and everything.

I thought about Bishop's guys names. Torch and Monty. As compared to Duke's right hand man, Chris. Torch and Monty sounded like trouble. Both were quiet and very business-like. I also noticed when Bishop was in their presence, he was different—more authoritative, which added to his allure. It was like they knew who was in command. It was then I realized it wasn't nervous energy—the SUV was filled to the rooftop with confidence. Confidence that only dangerous men could display in dangerous situations.

When we got to the neighborhood, I instructed Torch to drive pass the block first so we could see who was out and about. But most importantly, I wanted to see if there was a threat out there. Sure, Diamond had a couple of haters out there who'd love to see her fall. But she also had a few niggas who'd at least call the cops for her if they saw that she was in danger. I knew for a fact that if that Rodney cat was out there, that he'd assist in catching that bitch off guard.

As we cruised through the 'hood to check out the scenery, I didn't see anyone who'd pose a threat to us. And when I looked over at Diamond's apartment I could also see there were two sets of lights on in her apartment, which led me to believe that she was there. Now I couldn't say for sure if she had any guest in there with her, but at least I felt confident enough to let Bishop know that we were on to something.

"I'm not sure how long she's going to be in there, but I do know that she is there," I told him.

"Is there anywhere around here that we can park without bringing attention to ourselves?" Torch asked.

"Yeah, go around the block," I said. "We can park on the back street. We won't be able to see her entire apartment. But we'll be able to see her if she tries to leave out of her front door."

"A'ight," Torch said.

"No," Bishop said. Torch stopped the truck in the middle of the street. I was worried we would bring undue attention our way. "Fuck that, Torch. We are going in the front door. Lock and loaded. If that bitch ass nigga, Duke, or his boy, Chris, shoot this way and ask questions, I want him to know that Lynise and three badass niggas rolled up on his bitch's apartment and smacked her around."

I was speechless. What the fuck was he thinking? We should be keeping a low profile. And I didn't want to smack Diamond around, I wanted that bitch dead.

Torch parked the Escalade and I was thinking that this was bad. This fire ass whip would be jacked as soon as we were out of sight. Then something happened as we got out of the truck. One, we were all sporting black jackets, a white shirt and black slacks. Two, Bishop signaled me to lead the way. Three, and this was the thing that really fucked me up. As we walked, everyone who saw us had an immediate respect. We were four bad muthafuckas and everyone, including my cat, Rodney, saw us and knew not to fuck with us or our ride.

I had never felt this fucking powerful before. Bishop had put me in front for a reason. To stand big and walk tall. And I did. My chest was out, my confidence was high, my stride was long. This is the bitch I always wanted to be. And I had three real fucking men behind me who had my back.

It was then that I knew that no, I wasn't dying that night. Matter-of-fact, none of us were dying that night. We owned the fucking night. This was our night, our temporary territory. We were about to set this muthafucka on fire . . . and I was the ring leader. Hell yeah!

We made our way across the parking lot and up the stairs and no one said anything to us. I saw the respect, but I also saw the fear. And I loved that shit.

As we walked towards the door, I realized why Bishop and his boys had jackets on. They were strapped to the hilt with Glocks, Sig Sauers and I was sure I saw both Torch and Monty hiding Uzis under their jackets. And amazingly, we didn't break stride as all three guys pulled our guns in both hands.

As we approached the door, Bishop signaled to Torch to do his thing, which was kick the door in. When he did, Diamond was surprised as shit as she jumped up from the sofa. And even before she could scream, Monty pointed his Glock and told her to shut the fuck up. I was surprised as hell. That bitch's mouth was wide open and not a word came out.

I looked over at Bishop and he said, "For now, it's your show. Do what you have to do, but don't kill her. We need answers."

I didn't say anything as I walked to Diamond and when I was within two feet of that bitch, I threw a right hand that connected squarely on her nose. And suddenly I was Laila Ali in that bitch. I was throwing combinations—lefts and rights, rights and lefts. I was hitting her ass on top of her head, in her face, on her body. I had the power on my side. But more, I had the strength of revenge, the memories of a one-sided friendship, the thoughts of jail, the reminiscence of a family who didn't give a fuck about me . . . and lastly, the thoughts of a man, Duke Carrington, who had brought me to the lowest point in my life—with the help of my former best friend.

I was in kill mode and Diamond's nasty and grimy ass would have died then and there if Torch hadn't lifted me by my armpits and pulled me off that bitch.

It was then that I noticed the door was off its hinges. But Monty didn't stand in the doorway, he provided look out duties by looking out the curtains. These muthafuckas were serious. They knew what they doing. They were prepared for any and everything. And now I was one of them. Whether it be for a night, two nights or the rest of my life, I was one of them.

When I turned back around to look at Diamond, Bishop had his hand around her throat, lifting her up. He threw her ass hard in a recliner near the television, opposite the wall where the couch set. It was a new recliner since I lived here.

UNIQUE

I got a look at her face and strangely as it was, I felt good. Her face was completely swollen from the beating I had given her monkey ass. Both of her eyes were completely shut. Her face was beet red. I think my first punch broke her nose as I noticed all of the blood from her nose as well as her busted lips.

And the good thing, I didn't feel any remorse.

That bitch tried to get me killed. And like Katrina, she picked the wrong fucking team.

Bishop was barraging her ass with a series of questions.

Did you set up Neeko to get killed?

Who killed him?

What part did you play in it?

Where was Duke hiding out?

Were Duke and Chris hiding out together?

I couldn't hear Diamond's answers. She was barely whispering. I had fucked her up just that much. It was then that I noticed my knuckles were red with blood on both my hands and probably sore, but I didn't feel the pain. I was high on adrenaline.

When Bishop was through interrogating her ass, he spat in her face. Damn, I was a sadistic bitch myself because I was loving this shit. This really was me. This was my world.

Bishop went in the kitchen and I heard water running. When he came out he had two wet rags. He wrapped both around my hands. Then he looked at Torch and nodded his head one time.

Torch took two steps towards Diamond and grabbed her head and made a hard twist. Just like that, her neck was snapped.

No gun, no bullet, no knife, no noise.

Just as we had walked to the apartment, we walked the same way back to the car. Bishop whispered in my ear as we approached the car. I signaled my cat, Rodney, over and I told him to spread the word to the folks around the area that was out tonight that this was done by Duke Carrington, the cat who always dropped Diamond off in the Porsche. Then I handed him a wad of cash. Bishop would tell me later the amount of the wad—twenty thousand. Hush money. It was Rodney's job to spread the money around and of course, keep half for himself.

Rodney knew the deal as did everyone else. They knew power when they saw it. And in the 'hood, money and power truly did talk. Even though they didn't know Bishop, whoever opened their mouth knew this powerful dude would come back and take them out. And if he was in a bad mood, he would probably take out the whole family as well.

As we departed the apartment's parking lot, I thought about the good and bad times Diamond and I had together. We were girls. I loved that bitch for most of my life. She was my girl, my bitch. She was my ride and die forever. And the bitch betrayed me—and for what, a no-good ass nigga who didn't give a fuck about me, her or anyone else.

You chose wrong, bitch. You chose wrong.

UNIQUE

One Down, Two to Go

L *oyalty has been known to die a hard and painful death.*
Torch took his time departing that wretched ass neighborhood as if we were cruising the park after freshly waxing a car. I didn't get these cats. You would think we were just chilling on a Friday or Saturday night. My adrenaline was pumping hard through my entire body and I was ready for what was to come next. But I still didn't get these cats.

Bishop gave Monty the address to program the GPS to where Chris was hiding out. When he said Lake Edwards Drive, I knew we were headed to the Lake Edwards area. Lake Edwards was considered the 'hood. The townhouses out there were built in the early eighties and back then it was considered a middle class neighborhood. Now those same houses were worn down from all the bad tenants and wannabe drug pushers that plagued the streets of the neighborhood. I wanted to ask Bishop why Chris would be in Lake Edwards. I was sure Diamond told him. If she answered all of his questions, which I was sure she did, then he also knew where Duke was hiding out. But truthfully, I realized it didn't even matter at this point. So I said fuck it as I sat back and took in the scenery.

Torch entered Lake Edwards from Newtown Road, near a 7-Eleven convenience store. My heart picked up speed the closer we came to the address Chris was reportedly at. I was shocked to see that the streets were deserted. This wasn't how this place normally was. Something just wasn't right. Either the police had just rolled through and did a sweep or we were walking into an ambush. Damn, I wished I could put my finger on it. But I couldn't, so I warned Bishop and his two men to keep their heads up. And after they assured me that they would, I said a quiet prayer. I had a feeling that God wouldn't want to hear a word I had to say, especially after what I did to Diamond. But I figured what could it hurt to talk to Him anyway? He was the ruler of all the earth. And nothing would happen unless He signed off on it. So who better to go to but the source?

I had to get in focus. I was losing perspective. Thoughts of that trick, Diamond, were shooting in and out of my head. Good times and bad were playing ping pong in my brain. One thought was of us as kids and pre-teens, playing hop-scotch and jacks. Other thoughts were of us growing up to be teenagers and doing all kinds of foul shit that pissed off our teachers, parents and any other authority figure we could piss off. Then there were the memories of me always trying to save her grimy ass from this situation or that situation—from some nigga wanting

UNIQUE

to kick her ass for her stealing from him to a mad wife tired of Diamond fucking her husband. In the long run, that didn't make a bit of difference either, that bitch deserved to die. And most importantly, she deserved the ass whipping I gave her.

By the time we arrived at the residence Diamond said Chris would be, Bishop's Blackberry started vibrating. It was easy to hear. The radio was on a jazz satellite station and turned down low. Bishop looked down at the caller ID, and I shot a look as well. The name on the phone display was *Wifey*.

Fuck me! For whatever reason, an instant and sharp pain shot through my heart. I literally wanted to take the phone out of his hand and tell that bitch to go and get a life. This was my time with Bishop, not hers, so why the fuck couldn't she stay in her own lane. Shit, he would be back in New Jersey soon, so stop sweating him while he was here. It was at that time that I realized I wanted the fairy tale. I wanted this muthafucka to come swinging down on a vine and sweep me off my feet and take me away from this wasteland forever because I did not deserve to be here.

Yep, I realized snatching the phone from Bishop would not have gone over well. Not with Bishop, nor with the men who sat in the front seat as his bodyguards and protectors. So I sat back and waited to see how he would handle this awkward situation.

"Drive around the block one more time," Bishop instructed Torch and then he pressed the send button. "What's up, baby?" he said to her.

I had to be honest and say I was about to flip out, because I had become jealous. The way he said *baby* had a lot of meaning behind it. I'd never had a man talk to me like that. And what was even worse was he said it like he meant it. Thank God I couldn't hear what she said on the other end, because I knew her voice alone would probably irritate me.

Quite honestly, this was messing me up. Bishop being on the phone supposed to be an awkward moment for him, but it wasn't. It was awkward for me, considering my feelings. I was sure this was normal, everyday business for him. But for me the awkwardness spoke volumes. We were about to probably commit murder again and this muthafucka was talking to his bitch on the phone. I wonder if there was even a morsel of regret for what he did to Diamond.

Shit! I had to get a grip. In my heart I was acting as if Bishop belonged to me or I was his lady. The hug when we saw each other again and the clothes and food at the hotel had given me a false sense of reality. The truth was I wanted his ass. I wanted him to treat me like the bitch he was talking to. The inflection in his voice had changed. He was gentle with her, whoever she was, and more attentive. In any other man it would probably come off as a sign of weakness. With Bishop, it only added to his strength. He really was the epitome of powerful in so many ways.

"Nah, I won't be able to do that right now. But I could probably do it early in the morning," he told her and then he fell silent.

UNIQUE

While Bishop spoke calmly with his worrisome ass woman, I turned my attention towards the houses and the trees we passed in the neighborhood. I tried to block his conversation out, but it was very difficult to do. Finally, after three long and agonizing minutes, he ended his call. And boy was I happy about that.

"Come on, let's get down to business," Bishop said and I knew the meaning in his words, *Let's hurry up and do what we have to do so we can get out of here.*

Torch drove slowly back down Lake Edwards Drive and we noticed a white late model Honda Accord had pulled up in front of the address Diamond gave Bishop. Monty pointed it out.

"Yeah, I see that," Bishop replied.

"Do you want me to stop or keep going?" Torch wanted to know.

"Pull up about three or four houses behind the parked car," Bishop instructed.

"Maybe I should pretend I'm going to go knock on someone's door," I suggested. Bishop liked that idea. When I was about to step out of the truck, both the passenger and driver side doors opened on the Honda Accord. Bishop put his hand on my shoulder as if he was telling me to hold on.

We all watched as a young black woman stepped out of the driver side, while a tall cat hopped out of the passenger side, with an Applebee's carryout bag in his hand. I couldn't believe our stroke of luck. I knew that big muthafucka anywhere. It was Chris. Both luck and coincidence were on our side. "That's him. That's Chris right there," I blurted out.

Bishop looked at me. "Are you sure?"

"Fuck yeah, I'm sure!" I spit out. "He's wearing the exact same thing he was wearing last night and even if he wasn't, I know that muthafucka anywhere."

Bishop didn't say another word. He touched Torch on the back of his shoulder and without saying a word, Torch knew to drive up directly behind the car.

These fucking guys and their non-verbal communication were amazing. They were poetry in motion and the only thing I needed to do was follow in their footsteps.

When Torch punched the gas and pulled up behind the Honda, all three men jumped out in unison, and bum rushed Chris and his lady. "I want both of them in the house," I heard Bishop say.

"What do you want me to do?" I called out to him.

"You coming with us," he said in a fading voice.

Within seconds they were in the face of Chris and his lady. This shit reminded me of some gang wars. It was surreal. I couldn't believe that I was yet in another sting operation to take down another one of Duke's flunkies. I couldn't wait to see Chris's face when he saw me. That shit would be priceless.

The sudden bum rush on Chris and his female companion caught them both off guard. I didn't get it. This son-of-a-bitch really wasn't on the lookout for anyone assaulting his criminal ass. He should have known either the cops or somebody would be after his sorry ass. After all, it was over the news that Duke Carrington and his bodyguard, Chris Washington, was wanted in the murder of Katrina.

UNIQUE

When Chris's female companion saw Bishop and his boys coming at them with their guns aimed and cocked, she screamed instantly. Torch pointed his gun directly into her face and demanded she shut the fuck up or else. Chris dropped the carryout bag and tried to make a run for it, but little Monty got to him before he could move an inch. My heart raced as I watched everything unfold. I swear it was like watching an episode of *Fugitives.*

"Get 'em in the house," Bishop instructed Torch who had the female in his grasp.

I watched how Monty and Bishop handled Chris, while Torch forced the chick towards the front door. "Is anybody in the house?" he asked her as she fumbled to get her keys out.

She whimpered a barely audible no.

"You better not be lying to me," he threatened her.

I looked around at the other townhouses on the street. I had to make sure no one was watching us. At this point in the game, we didn't need any interruptions. Not the police, or anyone else. But as I thought about it, if someone did see us, they would probably put a deaf ear and blind eye to what we were doing. If they knew Chris or anything about him, they probably thought he was getting what he deserved. Anyway, when I felt the coast was clear, I focused my attention back on Bishop and Monty as they forced Chris into the house behind Torch and the woman.

Before I entered the house behind them, I looked around at all the windows and front doors once more. This was the least I could do in a situation like this.

"Lynise, get your ass in here now!" I heard Bishop yell. I turned around and rushed into the house, making sure I didn't touch the door handle with my hands. I used the bottom part of my jacket to open the door, because I knew I couldn't leave a single fingerprint, especially after what Bishop came here to do.

Inside the house, I closed door and locked it behind me. Shit was already heating up very quickly. When Chris saw my face, he looked like he saw a motherfucking ghost. I smiled at his bitch ass while Bishop and Monty had him cornered at the end of the sofa with their guns aimed directly at his fucking face.

"Thought your bitch ass was going to get me last night, huh?" I said. "Well, the joke is on you playa!" I put emphasis on the last word for his bitch ass. But he didn't respond. I started to spit on his ass but I couldn't take the risk of leaving my DNA on this bastard. That didn't stop me from punching him in his fucking face. *SMACK!* I tried to take his fucking nose off. "You ain't nothing but a fucking flunky," I continued. "Around here doing Duke's dirty work. Now look at your dumb ass! Too bad your existence on this earth is about to expire."

I laughed at his stupid ass and it felt good. So, so good. Fuck him. And fuck Diamond too. Both of these dumbasses deserved to die for being flunkies for big and powerful Duke Carrington.

"Fuck you bitch! If I had the chance I'll try to kill your ass again," he roared as spit shot out of his mouth.

Monty and Bishop looked at each other. "That nigga got heart!" Torch laughed.

UNIQUE

I agreed. "Yeah, he sure does. But let's see how much heart that muthafucka got after he bleeds too death," I commented.

"No, please don't kill 'em. We got a family!" his lady cried out.

Torch's hand wrapped around her neck incredibly fast that I didn't see where it came from. I had never seen someone move so fucking fast. "Shut the fuck up before you get it first!" he warned her.

She didn't say another word but tears rolled down her face like a waterfall.

"Y'all bitch ass niggas do me in. She ain't got shit to do with what I do," Chris blurted out.

Bishop smacked the back of Chris's head with the butt of his pistol. Blood skirted everywhere. "Casualty of war," Bishop said in a smooth and mellow tone. "See Mr. Washington, when you kill another person's family member, you have to expect the same."

I watched Chris's expression after Bishop hit him with his gun. From what I could surmise, that pain hit him hard. All he did was suppress his scream and hold the back of his head. No, that was the physical pain and he could take that. What was getting to him was the mental anguish Bishop was putting him through. He had all but told Chris that his lady was dying tonight. I didn't react to that, but I really didn't know what to feel about that. I didn't know the bitch. But she was with Chris and knew who Chris worked for, so she had to have some idea how foul he was. If she wasn't a casualty of war, she was indeed a casualty of stupidity.

CHEAPER *to* KEEP HER 2

"Christopher," Bishop continued but hesitated as if he was letting the sound of Chris's formal name resonate with him. "You don't mind if I call you by the name on your birth certificate, do you?" Chris didn't say anything in return but his eyes were tight, red and full of venom. "I have found that men of danger like us . . . have one very big problem . . . we don't account for family. Our families. We think we are indestructible . . . therefore, our families are protected by our bravado and reputation." Once again Bishop stopped and let his words sink in.

I liked his moments of hesitation. That shit sent a message and somehow drove the point home.

I didn't understand. Bishop was smooth as hell. But what was killing me was he was taking his time, like we were at a friend's house holding a nice casual conversation. What if someone did see us and had the balls to come do us in? What if this was a huge set-up and Duke and his other men would be here soon?

It was also at that moment that I noticed the Applebee's carryout bag in the house. I didn't know who had brought the bag in. But it was my first time seeing the silencer on Monty's weapon.

"Tell me where Duke is at?" Bishop said.

Chris's look at Bishop grew more intense. I thought it was the angriest expression he could muster up. "Nigga, if I knew I wouldn't tell you. So do what you gotta do and stop wasting my motherfucking time!" he barked. I prayed that stupid muthafucka didn't have more loyalty to Duke than he did to his lady and their kids. Was he really willing to make his kids parentless? At least Bishop may have mercy on his female companion.

UNIQUE

"As you wish," Bishop replied and then he pulled back on the chamber of his Glock.

"Wait, I know where he is," the woman blurted out. But before she was able to say another word, the doorbell rang. Fear crept in my heart at that very moment. My first thought was to run out the back door because I knew without a doubt that it was the police. Someone from the neighborhood saw us force Chris and his girlfriend into the house and now they were here to save them. I swear I didn't know whether to surrender or go all out with Bishop and do a shout-out.

When the doorbell rang a second time, I got even more nervous. Everybody including Bishop stood still. Then the woman whispered, "It's probably my neighbor, Tracy. She called me earlier to see if she could borrow a pair of my shoes."

Bishop looked at Torch and nodded his head. Another one of those non-verbal commands from Bishop that Torch evidently knew what it meant.

"Don't try anything stupid," I heard Torch say to her in a low voice.

"I promise I won't," she assured him.

"Just ask who is it?" he instructed her.

She did as told and indeed it was her neighbor. Torch told her to open the door as Bishop walked over to the door as well. Bishop got behind the lady, while Torch repositioned himself next to the door. I looked over at Chris, in fear that he would try something stupid, but Monty had his gun with the silencer pointed at his head. I knew if Chris even attempted to shout out, he would probably be dead within a split second. I also noticed that

Monty didn't look up or anything. He was a true professional. His eyes were glued on Chris.

When Chris's girlfriend opened the door and with a blinding quickness, Torch reached out and grabbed the neighbor Tracy by his hair and pulled her in the house. I couldn't fucking believe it, another fucking witness.

Fuck! Another casualty of war!

UNIQUE

You Go To Hell First

*W**hat becomes of a broken heart?***
I felt bad for the little girl that was unfortunately caught up in a mess that she didn't know anything about. I knew the girl. I had seen her around at several of the clubs. I knew she was also a stripper at several of the clubs throughout the area. She was very attractive like Chris's girlfriend but she carried just a little more weight around the hip area and she wore a ton of hair weave. Any moron would know that her hair wouldn't be that long and straight when her roots needed a touch up. She also looked like a child so I assumed she was probably in her mid-twenties—much too young to die.

After Torch was sure no one was waiting on her at her house, he sat both women down on the sofa, opposite the chair that Chris was in. He then asked Chris's chick did she have any duct tape in the house and she said no in a low voice.

Bishop signaled for Monty to go search the house to see if he could find something to probably tie the women up with and that's when things suddenly jumped off.

Monty took two steps backward with his gun still aimed at Chris's head, while Bishop was walking back over to Chris's position. For whatever stupid heroic reason, Chris took this as an advantage to strike back. He lunged at Bishop but Monty shot him in his right knee and he cried out. Chris's chick screamed and Torch backhanded her so hard, she passed out. Meanwhile her friend, Tracy, bolted for the door, but Monty shot her in the head from across the room.

If everything didn't jump off so fast I would have probably screamed myself. I was so happy I didn't. I certainly didn't want to be a casualty of war as well.

When I looked back around at Chris, Bishop had stuffed a hamburger in his mouth to keep him from yelling out. I was surprised they never tied up Chris's hands but I wouldn't be surprised if they wanted him to do something wrong anyways. I played it off but I knew Bishop already had Duke's location. He got that from Diamond. I understood if he was trying to verify her information but something told me that Diamond was too afraid to lie to us.

But I looked at everything that had just happened and there was only one word I could think of—efficient. These muthafuckas really were a well-oiled, smooth machine. Bishop had everything under control. Poor Tracy was the innocent one and she had died within two minutes of being in the house. And Chris's chick was out like a light for now. Torch was looking out the window to make sure everything was cool and considering it was past midnight, it was cool.

Bishop pulled the coffee table over and sat in front of Chris. "It's not too late to save your girl, the mother of your children," he said. "Honestly, is Duke Carrington worth all of that?"

Chris was still writhing in pain. He was also trying to eat as much of the hamburger as he could to keep from gagging. What was left of the hamburger, Bishop finally took out of his mouth. I think it was an unsaid command that if Chris tried screaming he was a dead man.

This was the first time I actually saw tears in Chris's eyes. And I don't think it was from the pain. I noticed he kept trying to see what was going on with his chick.

"Christopher, forget Duke for now," Bishop got his attention with those words. "I just want to know if Neeko suffered when y'all killed him."

The question surprised Chris, as well as me. Chris stopped writhing and moving around. His eyes dropped to the floor. The tears fell faster and heavier.

"Or should I say . . . when you killed him." There it was—the eight hundred pound gorilla in the room. What this was all about. "You know, Chris, I am so close to letting you go, especially since you don't have a knee now, and just killing Shakira over there."

Chris looked up and his face was all fucked up. Snot was running from his nose, the tears and pain had turned his eyes beet red and the anger still persisted on his face. But I know what this was all about. Bishop knew his lady's name. Hell, I didn't know the bitch's name. That one fact had fucked up the big man.

CHEAPER *to* KEEP HER 2

"Yeah, I know, Christopher," Bishop said matter-of-factly. "Shakira Dalton. Sweet girl. The mother of your three kids: Christopher Junior, LaShunda, named after your cousin who died in a drive-by when you guys were ten years old, and Connor, named after your uncle who raised you."

I didn't know what was fucking with Chris more. The fact that Bishop had obviously done his homework and knew shit Chris never thought he should have known. Or the fact this muthafucka was still speaking in the calmest and smoothest voice while he was putting the screws to him. If it was me, I would just want his ass to shut up or at least raise his voice so I could know how pissed off he was at me.

This cat was truly scary. I remembered Neeko telling me on several occasions that he had a family member that he was convinced was psycho. But he loved him to death. He never told me it was his own brother, just a family member like it could be a cousin or uncle or something. He said he remembered this family member talking to a girl and this dude rolled up on them and wanted to start some shit because it was his girl. Evidently the family member thought it was the girl's decision to make. She chose him. When the other dude objected and he and his two friends tried to jump Neeko's family member, Neeko said in less than a minute all three dudes were on the ground with bloody noses, swollen eyes, busted lips and wounded prides.

And during all of this, the family member would speak in the most calm and soothing voice. I knew now Bishop was that family member. What he was doing when he was younger, he was now doing on a larger scale when he was older.

Chris was outclassed and outgunned. He had a choice. Choose his family over his boss and probably best friend or vice versa. I really hope he would choose his family.

"I'm sorry," I heard Chris say. The words were slurred but he mustered up the strength to say it with conviction. I was sure he did that to save his family.

"Yeah, you are," Bishop replied. "You are and so am I."

Suddenly the tears ran down Chris's face like he was spouting a new river. "No, no, no," he repeatedly said.

Torch threw water in Shakira's face to wake her up. Then he told her to stand up. Chris was still voicing his rejection in the form of *no, no, no.* Bishop rose to his feet. He took out the gun that was in its holster in the inside of his jacket. It also had a silencer on the tip of the barrel.

"Diamond's dead," Bishop said to Chris. The big man just kept saying *no* repeatedly. "An eye for an eye, motherfucker." With that Bishop pointed the gun at Shakira and pulled the trigger. The bullet went directly into Shakira's left eye and out the back of her head, shattering her brain. There was nothing there but parts of flesh and blood. Chris once again tried to jump up and this time Monty shot him in the other knee. Chris fell to the floor writhing in more pain. The pain wouldn't last long.

While he suffered on the floor in pain of both the mental and physical kind, Bishop stood over Chris and say, "This is for my brother, Neeko!" Then he squeezed the trigger. BOOM! BOOM! Pop! Pop! Bishop emptied two shots to the back of Chris's head. The silencer suppressed the sound. Chris's lifeless body fell limp as the blood slowly oozed out of his head.

Once a criminal always a criminal!

THE HUNT IS ON

What a woman desires—a man will always deliver.

I tried to take in everything around me. I looked at Chris's dead body as blood oozed from his head. Then I looked at Tracy, Chris's girlfriend's neighbor. Out of all the lifeless bodies in the room, I felt sorry for her. All she wanted to do was borrow a pair of Shakira's stiletto heels. And now she and Shakira were both dead because of some bullshit Chris did. This whole scenario was mind blowing and I knew that it was just the beginning.

Bishop signaled Torch and Monty to head out. They had to step over Tracy's body and Bishop and I followed suit. We all made sure we didn't step in the puddle of blood surrounding her head after Bishop warned us not to do it. And when we finally got outside, these dudes took their fucking time getting the fuck out of dodge. I didn't get that shit. Were they that fucking confident that no one would blow the whistle on their asses?

CHEAPER *to* KEEP HER 2

"Where to next?" Torch asked after he got back in the driver seat and started up the ignition.

Bishop looked down at his watch. "We still got time," he said. Then he gave Torch the address to where he was told Duke would be. Torch headed back up Lake Edwards Drive and made a quick right turn on Newtown Road. When he arrived at the intersection of Virginia Beach Boulevard and Newtown Road, he shot straight across Virginia Beach Boulevard and jumped on Highway 264.

We were heading towards the city of Chesapeake, near the North Carolina border. That part of Chesapeake was very secluded. In fact, it was so secluded that the closest hospital and police precinct was at least fifteen to twenty miles away. The nickname for this part of Chesapeake was known as Death Valley, with its beautiful with brand new million dollar homes build on ten acres of land. The name didn't fit the area but supposedly it was named that because if you had a serious medical emergency and had less than ten minutes to live, then you were good as gone. Other than that, living out in this area was like living the high life.

The ride to Death Valley but also known as Pelican Estates, took at least thirty-five minutes. And when we finally arrived in the area, Bishop realized that it was too dark to maneuver. Each house was built on its own land like the plantations of old. You had to drive down long dirt roads to get to each person's house, so it would be very easy for them to see when they had unwelcomed visitors.

UNIQUE

When the GPS indicated that Duke's residence was less than a half-mile away, Bishop instructed Torch to pull to the side of the road and turn the headlights off. Then he told Monty to hand him the night vision binoculars from the glove compartment. Right after Monty handed the binoculars to Bishop, Bishop pressed the red button on the left side of the binoculars and then he placed them right before his eyes. He scanned the entire property that was about a half- mile ahead of us, while everyone including me, waited for him to speak.

Finally, he took the binoculars away from his eyes and said, "I see three cars parked out in the driveway but I don't see any lights on in the house. So I've got a few concerns."

"You know whatever call you make, I'm with it," Monty assured him.

"Yeah, just tell us what you want us to do," Torch said.

I sat back and watched as both of Bishop's men waited for him to give them further instructions. The power and the strength he carried in his voice sent chills down my spine. There was no question in my mind that he was in control.

"I think it's gonna be difficult to get to him tonight because he has security cameras on each corner of his house and the outside of the house is lit up with extra lighting. It wouldn't surprise me if he had motion detectors around his house too, so I think it's best if we go back to the hotel and re-group. We can't risk fucking this mission up just because we want him that bad."

"Cool, I agree," Monty replied.

CHEAPER *to* KEEP HER 2

"Yeah, me too," Torch sounded off and then he put the truck in reverse to turn around. After he felt like he backed the truck up far enough, that's when he turned it around and flicked back on the headlights.

As we drove away I turned around in my seat to look back at the house Duke was supposedly in and I became so frustrated that we weren't going to be able to snatch his ass up tonight. I wanted so badly to see him squirm and beg for his life while Bishop, Torch and Monty tortured him to death. It seemed as if I had waited for this day for a very long time and now it wasn't going to happen when I expected it to. I agreed with Bishop that this wasn't a good time to go inside Duke's house but with all the added security that motherfucker had protecting him, when would be the right time? I wanted his ass got now. I wanted him to feel all the fucking pain I endured behind him. I also wanted him to reap all the shit he did to all of those innocent young women who were killed and had their babies taken from them.

After all, he deserved it.

Duke was a fucking heartless monster. I mean, who marries their fiancée and then have them killed not even a month later so they can collect on their life insurance policy? I bet she thought without a shadow of doubt that he loved her and would jump in the line of fire for her. That's the way he came across. That motherfucker was very charismatic. He'd talk a bitch into selling her pussy to her own daddy. I couldn't put my finger on it but it wouldn't surprise me if Duke worked some type of roots or witchcraft on us. Virginia and other states further in the south lived off that voodoo shit. I just wished I had a

UNIQUE

way of finding out. He'd pay triple for the shit he took me through.

On our way back to the hotel I couldn't get my mind off the fact that we were leaving this bastard to live life a few more hours. Bishop saw how disgusted I was and tapped me on my knee. "Don't worry about it. We're gonna get 'em," he told me.

When the words penetrated my mind I felt just a little better. I guess I needed to be reassured in some way, form or fashion. Bishop seemed as if he was a man of his word so I took it for what it was worth and accepted it.

After we arrived back at the hotel, Bishop handed me the hotel room key and told me he'd join me later. I knew he was going into Monty and Torch's room to discuss how they'd be able to get to Duke. I wanted to join in on the discussion with them but I figured I'd let them handle it. Besides, I had no knowledge of dodging security cameras and motion sensors. So I did what I was told and went into the room.

It didn't take Bishop long to join me. I thought he'd be with Monty and Torch at least a couple of hours but he came back about thirty minutes later. I had already taken a shower and was tucked away inside the sheets when he sat on the bed. I looked at him and smiled because this was the first time in many years that I felt this safe. Not only did he possess the physical attributes, his swagger was out of this world. The way he looked at me made me want to melt. I was a very attractive woman myself. And my body was in tip-top shape and I didn't have any stretch marks. Neeko used to beg me to hop on stage when he was alive. He knew niggas would line up to see my body. I had a very tiny waist and ass, and my hips were to die for. Plus, my titties were perky so I never owned a push-up bra. Yes, I was a bad bitch in my own right. I just needed a good man to appreciate me.

He didn't say anything. Instead he grabbed the TV remote and started flipping through the channels. When he found a local channel that had the news on, he stopped. It was past three in the morning and the newscast was a rebroadcast. However, the news ticker was scrolling across the bottom of the screen. I stopped and read it just like Bishop was doing.

Breaking News: The Virginia Beach and Norfolk Police Departments are in search of local business man Duke Carrington and his bodyguard, Christopher Washington, for the suspected murder of Katrina Bishop of Virginia Beach, and a female victim in Norfolk that the local authority are not releasing her name yet.

I shook my head at the craziness of it all. I wonder how Diamond would have felt knowing she was known as the *female victim in Norfolk.* They could have at least said her name. But I was just happy Rodney had spread the word to blame Duke for the killing of Diamond. I hoped Rodney would also do something good with the money besides buy more product to sell on the street. I knew his family could use the money. Hell, what family in the 'hood couldn't use money like that.

UNIQUE

Bishop evidently had seen everything he wanted to see as he turned the TV off. "I'm very proud of you," he said.

I really couldn't make heads or tails of what made Bishop tick. His voice inflection, his tone was the same as it was when we were taking care of business. He was just too cool for me.

"Thank you," I said in return. "I was nervous initially, but everything just fell into place after I beat the shit out of Diamond."

"You okay with that?" he asked. I could hear the concern in his voice and see it in his eyes.

"Yeah, why wouldn't I be," I added.

"She was your friend . . . not only that, your best friend for years. It's hard losing someone close to you . . . even if they betray you." He walked around the bed and sat right next to me, putting his hand on my cheek. I almost melted. His hand was warm and inviting. Not rough like I thought it would be. He was a hard brotha with a gentle touch. A rarity in the world I grew up in, the world I had known for most of my life.

"I'm doing good, thanks to you," I replied.

"I didn't do anything, Lynise, I just gave you wings. It was up to you to flap them and make them fly. I'm proud that you did that."

Then we just looked at each other and took in the moment. Neither one of us moved to make a move. I wondered what he was thinking. I was just hoping it was about me.

"We're gonna head back out to Duke's place early in the morning to see if we can get him when he comes out.

That seems to be the only way we can get to him," he told me. That surprised me. I was hoping his next words would be, *I want you.*

"What time?" I played off my disappointment.

"I want to be out of here right before the sun comes up. I don't want to miss the chance of letting him leave the house and we're not there."

"Well, I think that's a good time because he does get up early."

Bishop looked down at his wristwatch. "Get some sleep. We only have four hours before we leave back out," he said as he started taking off his shoes.

Now, as bad as I wanted to get some sleep, I also wanted him to take me into his arms. I had to have him tonight. After he had taken off his shoes, I watched him take off his shirt, revealing a white t-shirt and then he slid out of his pants. I swear I was about to fucking cum on myself when I saw the print of his dick through his boxer shorts. It reminded me of the scene from the movie *Takers,* when Idris Elba got out of his bed in his boxers. Oh my God! Bishop's dick had to be the same exact size as Idris Elba. And I couldn't allow myself to lay there and not put it to good use. So as soon as he got into the bed with me I asked him if he could hold me.

"You sure you want me to do that?" he smiled.

I smiled back and said, "Yes, I'm sure."

We were laying in the fetal position and I loved every minute of it. And before I knew it his dick started rising to the occasion. My pussy got so warm and wet, it started pulsating. The feeling was incredible but I knew I needed to feel Bishop inside me to get the full effect. Knowing

UNIQUE

he had a woman back in New Jersey was shifted to the back of my mind. I didn't give a fuck about her at this point. Her man was in bed with me and I was going to take advantage of it. Plus, I figured if I fucked him good enough, he'd want to leave her ass for good.

"Damn, your dick is so hard," I commented while I massaged his hard manhood from behind. I did this so I could measure the size of it with my hand. And after I found out that my hand couldn't cover his entire penis, I became more excited. I was so excited that I turned my body completely around towards him and then I leaned in to kiss him. Oh my God! His lips were so soft and full. We were rotating our lips as we kissed each other passionately. Luckily for him I was completely naked. I knew that this was bound to happen which was why I decided not to slip on a pair of panties. I believed I took Bishop by surprise when he realized I was naked. But when he started licking and sucking on my nipples, it made things all better.

Not too much longer after he licked and played with my breast, he slid down my body. His soft kisses and licks on my stomach were only making me hotter. He was active and like everything else in his life, he was smooth. His hands were working their way up and down my body while his mouth teased me. When his mouth found my pussy and started teasing my clit with his tongue, I was in heaven. I was so fucking surprise when his tongue initially touched my clit, that I lifted my back and with both hands, I grabbed the back of his head and pushed his face in all of my wetness.

Granted, I was already wet so when he dug his tongue deep inside me, it became more pleasurable. I was bucking and humping his face like my mind was going bad. The feelings I felt with each touch were indescribable. "Oooooowww, yeah Bishop, lick right there," I instructed him. Damn, I loved a man who loved eating pussy and knew what he was doing. And this bastard knew what in the fuck he was doing. He was so good I could feel my toes twisting in all different directions. This shit was affecting my whole body. His hands went under my ass and I could feel the saliva running down the crack of my head.

"Wait, don't move. Stay right there," I demanded as I concentrated on climaxing. While he was eating my pussy like he was at a Japanese buffet, I was thinking about this sex tape I saw a while back with this chick sitting on this guy's face. She was grinding her pussy in his face and he was taking it all in. Thinking about how she was throwing her pussy at that other guy helped me explode all my juices into Bishop's mouth. I trembled while his face was buried between my thighs and his hands were pushing my ass more into his face. Damn, damn, damn! I think I had a double orgasm. This muthafucka was not stopping. He was eating my pussy like it was his last meal, like he was the muthafucka locked up and had just gotten out of jail.

Immediately after I exhaled, I grabbed him and pulled him on top of me. "I want you to fuck me!" I commanded. Without saying a word he pushed his entire dick inside of my pussy. And as he slid his dick deep inside of me, I began to feel like we were one. I know this sounds

UNIQUE

crazy but I was falling in love with this guy. The way he handled me while he thrust himself in and out of me was mind blowing. I couldn't get myself together. I felt like I was on cloud nine or in la-la land. The way he penetrated me was so gentle and passionate. He was literally making love to me. And the way he looked into my eyes left me in a trance.

"Hmmmm, this pussy is so wet and tight. I love this wet pussy!" he told me as he continued to thrust himself in and out of me.

I wanted him to know I was feeling him so I pulled his face to mine and started kissing more passionately. Yeah, he was a real man. Real men love it when a woman kisses them after they just ate her pussy. Real men loved it when a woman wasn't all prudish and shit, and didn't mind tasting herself. "Oh yeah, fuck me harder!" I said between kisses. And he happily obliged.

He put my legs over his shoulder and then he started long stroking me. He would look down at how hard he was fucking me and then he looked into my face to see my expression. I couldn't lie, this shit was feeling damn good. But I knew if I didn't express that physically or verbally, he wouldn't perform as well. That's just a man's ego. They want to know that they are doing their thing, so I made sure he knew it tonight.

"Damn right, fuck this pussy, baby. Fuck this pussy hard!" I told him. The more I talked nasty to him, the better he performed and about forty seconds later, he pulled his dick and squirted every ounce of cum his dick could produce. And while he was dropping it all over my pussy,

I was wiping it up with my index finger and then I'd lick it off.

He smiled at me and said, "I love the whore in you."

I smiled back and said, "You just don't know that that was just the beginning. I have a lot more tricks in my bag."

He didn't respond to that comment, but he did kiss me on my forehead, so that was good enough for me.

After our fucking session was over, he and I both washed ourselves off and jumped back into bed. He went out like a light. But it took me at least another twenty minutes to doze off. I couldn't get the way I felt about Bishop off my mind. I just hoped that I didn't play myself by fucking him too soon. And I knew that in time I would know.

UNIQUE

STRENGTH AND POWER

*W*hoever said men have the biggest balls—*lied!*
I couldn't remember the last time I had felt so damn good. There is nothing like a good man with a bank account, status and a horse dick. Better yet, there was nothing like a man who knew how to use that plywood between his legs as well as use his tongue as a weapon. That was exactly what Bishop had done—attacked me with his weaponry, and I was all the more better for it. I was on my cloud and it was much higher than cloud nine.

I felt good for only two or three hours of sleep. When I looked over at the clock, it read 11:30. I immediately jumped up and fumbled over myself.

What the fuck!

I looked around and there was no sign of Bishop. I was about to run out the room when I saw the note taped to the TV screen.

*There's been a change of plans. We're going
back in tonight, so chill for now. I will be back
soon. Read the newspaper, very interesting article on your boy. But please stay in the room
because you are a wanted woman. Police
think you are Duke's accomplice. We will
handle that as well and exonerate your name.
See you when I get back.*

The first thing I had to say to myself was I trust this
man, he wouldn't fuck me like Duke had done. That
meant a lot. More importantly, I really had to believe
that. I had a good feeling about Bishop, but my past
didn't allow me to trust far.

Then I read the note again and I had to stop. Read the
newspaper. The police was thinking I was Duke's accomplice. Hold on. Shit! Were they real or fucking with
me? I knew immediately it was the two damn detectives
trying to flush me out. I had their cards and I was going
to call, but first I wanted to read the newspaper that Bishop had left me.

Duke had made front-page news and what a story it
was. It talked about the young girls he had killed and the
motive was he wanted their babies to sell to the highest
bidder, and the highest bidder was suspected to be some
rich people in the area. Then it talked about his connec-
tion to Neeko and the club, and how he was suspected in
the killings of both Neeko and Katrina, and blowing up
the club. The motive for that was the insurance money he
would receive from his wife dying in the club. Yes, they
even knew about his wife being in the club. Amazingly,

he had taken out the insurance on her long before they married—like six months ago.

Man, Duke was off the motherfucking hook. He was crazy as hell.

The article went on to talk about the police had the name of one of his known female accomplices, and they were on the lookout for her. She was the last one seen at the house of Katrina Bishop, and had lived in one of four condos or townhouses that Duke Carrington owned. The police had searched his condos, townhouses and evidently, three other residences he owned. They named the locations of the residences and none of them was the one in Chesapeake.

When I put the newspaper down, I was stunned. I didn't know if I was coming or going. I wanted to call the detectives and tell them I didn't have anything to do with any of this. But that would have been a mistake . . . and a lie. I had a hellava lot to do with this. I had beaten Diamond down, plus I was there when she was killed, and I had intimate knowledge of Katrina's death and the death of two innocent women because they knew Duke's flunky, Chris.

No, my name wasn't associated with Duke Carrington in any of this. But it was associated with death—in a major way.

For now I said fuck it.

I took another shower and got myself together. I tried on all of the clothes Bishop had bought me the day before. I felt like the Queen Bee. I thought about our moment in bed and the lovemaking, and damn, my pussy got wet all over again. Shit, I was hoping we had a chance to do that shit again before he left. But truthfully speaking, my mind was on leaving with him.

Around six o'clock that evening I started getting worried, plus I was hungry as hell. I had had a couple bags of chips and a drink the whole day, and I was extremely hungry now. I hadn't heard from Bishop. Once again, I was thinking he had bailed on me. It was the story of my life, people I gave a damn about bailing on me. I was anxious and the anxiety was kicking the shit out of me. I searched for the detectives business cards but for some reason I couldn't find it.

What the hell? What did I do with it?

I knew I had the card after I got out of the lake and I had it at Devin's place. Bishop! Shit, he had it and now I knew my ass was in trouble. And don't ask me why I did what I did next, but I started packing the luggage he had bought me that morning. I was getting out of here but I wasn't leaving my clothes. I didn't stop to think about how shallow that was.

But as I was packing, the door opened and it was Bishop, along with his boys, Torch and Monty. Bishop had food in his hand. I felt so relieved, even though I wasn't sure I would live to see another day.

"Going somewhere?" Bishop asked.

"I wasn't sure," I began. "I hadn't heard from you and I didn't know if you were alright. You know it was a wild night and my adrenaline is kicking my ass. Plus, I'm hungry as a starving bear in the woods."

"All is cool," he said.

He turned on the TV and let me eat. I felt bad not believing in Bishop, after all he had done for me in such a short time. Plus, I was sure there was no place on God's green earth that could save me from the man if he came looking for me. I was a wreck and I knew it. Trust issues would be the death of me. I just hope that death was not in the short-term future.

After I ate, Bishop dropped Detective Whitfield's card down on the table where I was eating. I didn't know what to say or think.

"This is what we are going to do," he said. "I want you to call Detective Rosenberg, and read what I wrote down here. I want you to read this first and get familiar with it. I also want you to do some improvising but improvise with the information I provide you. I will also be whispering in your ear what to say. Understand?"

I shook my head. I didn't completely get it, but I understood. So I read what I was to say. Bishop had even written down possible questions the detectives may ask and my answers to those questions. When I was completely confident with the game plan and script, he made the call on a phone that was hooked up to three other phones that was hooked up to some kind of device.

Detective Rosenberg answered on the first ring and stated his name. On my end I was on the speakerphone.

"Yes, this is Lynise, tell your partner, Detective Whitfield, to pick up on the other phone, and both of you listen to what I have to say."

The phone went silent for a minute and I realized Rosenberg was talking to his partner. Then they both were on the line.

"No sense in trying to trace the number," I stated. "First, the phone is a burner, secondly, it will be routed through at least three sites before you can a decent hone on my general location. Also, what I have to say, I don't think you want anyone else hearing. And lastly, I have at least fifteen minutes before that will occur, so listen and do what I say."

Even though I was reading off a script, I felt confident, like I was in charge.

"Lynise, you need to turn yourself in," Detective Whitfield said. "You are in a lot of trouble and we are the only people who can help you. Your friend, Diamond, is dead, Katrina is dead, Neeko is dead, do you want to be next."

"Shut the fuck up, Detective," I said. That was me, not the script. "This is the play, the only play," the script read. "This is the address Duke Carrington is held up. This is the house you guys don't know about." I gave him the address in Chesapeake. "This is what's going to happen. "First, you are going to get your guys and coordinate with the Chesapeake Department, and you guys will raid his home. That's a given. But I also expect you to call the radio and television stations I give you, and they will broadcast that you guys have found Duke Carrington and are breaching his house a minute before you guys knock down the doors. Understand?"

"No, we don't understand," Rosenberg weighed in. "What makes you think we are going to get radio and TV stations involved in taking down a murder suspect. Not going to happen, missy. Now, turn yourself in or you are going down with your boyfriend."

UNIQUE

I laughed to myself. I couldn't tell Rosenberg from Whitfield. And I loved it. It's always nice to see the true colors of a cop come out.

"Detective, both you and your partner have other two thousand shares in Carter Business Holding Incorporated. Shares neither one of you could afford. Yes, I think you guys will leak this story to the local news stations if you don't want Internal Affairs investigating you."

The phone went silent and I knew both men had their hands over the receiver and trying to decide what was the best way to go. Then Detective Whitfield came back on, "Lynise, if you fuck us on this, that's your ass and that's a promise."

"You have one hour, Detective. If I don't hear what I want to hear, I promise you, the e-mail I have drawn up will be sent to the Chief of Detectives, the police chief and every newspapers and radio and television station in this area, as well as an anonymous e-mail sent to the FBI. So Detective Whitfield, no, don't fuck with me. One hour, the clock is running."

Who said a bitch can't run the show?

Tick, Tick, Tick

*I*n the company of dangerous men—it was my lifelong
dream, but it was my destiny.
We packed the Escalade and got on the move after
that. Evidently Bishop had already given Torch and Monty the address to where we were going because the GPS
started talking to us as soon as we pulled out of the hotel
parking lot.

We were headed west as we jumped on I-64 headed
towards Hampton, Norfolk or Newport News, or something west of our current location. We had checked out of
the hotel and packed everything up. I also noticed we had
a black duffel bag that was full of weapons. We were
headed out and Bishop was really turning over Duke to
the cops. I wasn't sure because we were dressed similarly
to our outfits the night before.

The sun was already down and I didn't know the
game plan. I was sure I was the only one who didn't
know the plan.

UNIQUE

"Where we going? Are we still going to take Duke down?" I asked with genuine concern and worry in my voice.

"Chill, baby. Just enjoy the ride," Bishop said. So that's what I did.

When we went through the tunnel and then got off I-64 by the Hampton University exit, I definitely didn't know what was up. I looked around the area and tried to guess where we were going and I couldn't.

Then we finally rolled into the outskirts of downtown Hampton, in a warehouse district, I was completely lost. I had never been in this area before in all the years I had lived in the Tidewater/Virginia Beach area.

We pulled over before we reached our destination. The GPS said we were a quarter mile form our destination. But we were parked.

"What's up," I said.

"Duke wasn't at the Chesapeake home," Bishop began. "He has been hanging out here in this warehouse district. He has about three or four guys at the house in Chesapeake. His game plan was to call in anonymously tomorrow to the cops and while they were getting their shit together, he would escape via a private jet at the Norfolk airport."

"How you know all of this?" I asked.

"I have my ways," he said and smiled.

He gave me a 9mm Beretta for protection. He had at least three guns that I could see and a knife, while Torch and Monty were trapped to the hilt with guns and assault rifles. This shit was heavy. And yes, I was scared.

The area was darker than any normal area. I noticed the lights that surrounded the place were all out. When we reached the warehouse, I noticed there was an old, dark color Chevy Impala between the warehouse we were about to breach and the one next to it. Bishop had a mini-radio attached to his belt and I knew he was listening to one of the radio stations we had gave the detectives to inform me a minute before the breach was supposed to happen.

When he heard what he was looking for, we all went in the same door and immediately we spread out. I stayed with Bishop. And yes, I was scared as shit.

The warehouse was big. There was machinery all around the place. Also, it wasn't an open area warehouse. There were different rooms and office spaces, plus a big supply tool area that was inside a caged area. It was then I also noticed I was the only one without ear buds. The other three guys were communicating amongst themselves, and I couldn't hear what was going on.

I also realized I was the only one without night vision goggles. But I had Bishop and I felt safe.

Then we heard the gunshots and instead of running where the shots were coming from, Bishop had taken another route.

We still heard gunshots as we deliberately made our way to the area where the shots were coming from. I didn't know why we didn't take the more direct route. Then it dawned on me. We were coming in from the back, behind Duke.

Then I saw him. He was by an office area, the light was on. He had three handguns, two Uzis and a rifle that I would later learn was a Russian-made AK-47, and a ton of ammunition.

Bishop took off his goggles and some of his gear. He kept his weapons. He told me to stay put. He told me when the lights came on, to call out Duke's name. He smiled and told me everything would be okay. I smiled back. A reassuring smile. I had belief in this dude and I knew he had the same thing in me.

I had to admit. I was afraid. Bishop moved slowly, deliberately, with a purpose. Then the lights came on and I can only surmise he had told one of his guys to hit the switch.

As soon as the lights came on, I did as told. I showed myself and called, "Duke!" as loud as I could.

When he saw me, he turned in my direction, and this was followed by five quick shots. Except it wasn't Duke shooting at me or anyone else.

It was Bishop.

This muthafucka had shot Duke in the front bone of both legs, directly below the knees, plus he had two shots in his thighs, one in each thigh, very close to his groin, and the last shot was right below his neck and right above his Kevlar vest. Fuck! I had never seen shooting like this before. Bishop was Billy the Kid reborn.

When Duke was hit, he dropped the rifle he had in his hand. Bishop and his boys moved in fast. I was right on his heels. I had to see this. I wanted to get as close as I could.

The man wasn't dead.

No one said anything, until I did. "You know what, Mr. Carrington, you have never looked as attractive to me as you do now."

He tried to get the words out, but he couldn't. That last shot below his neck had fucked him up. I was sure he was trying to tell me to fuck off or go to hell.

"Duke, I will go to hell, but you are going first. And when you get there, which will be soon, tell Diamond and Chris that I said hello." I stopped while he took it in. Then I said, "By the way, meet Bishop. You remember, Neeko's brother, the one you thought you had blown up."

His eyes got bigger and a tear from his eye.

Bishop didn't say anything. When a slight smile came over Duke's face, Bishop aimed his gun at Duke's head to put the final bullet in that muthafucka's skull.

I beat him to it. I held the gun with both hands and before Bishop could squeeze the trigger, I fired off three shots—all to Mr. Duke Carrington's head.

Die muthafucka! This was for the girls who died for nothing, not knowing the faith of their children, and for Neeko and all the patrons and workers who had died at the club in the bombing.

And lastly, this was for me. It was cheaper to keep me, bitch!

UNIQUE

EPILOGUE

*T*his was just the beginning!
The phone rang three times, before a nice sounding young lady picked up, "Hello, Carter Business Holdings Incorporated," she said.

"An old friend calling for Anthony Carter," Bishop stated.

Evidently the young lady recognized Duke Carrington's phone number. The line was still opened when she said, "Mr. Carter, someone is calling you on Mr. Carrington's phone."

The phone went to music, meaning Bishop was on hold. Then when the phone was reconnected, a male's voice said, "Anthony Carter speaking."

"Why so formal, AC," Bishop said. The phone went silent as if Anthony "AC" Carter had heard a ghost. "If you are there, more than likely, TC is right next to you. Am I right?"

"Without a doubt, you are definitely right," the hoarse voice of Terrence "TC" Carter replied. "How in the hell are you Bishop? It's been a while. When was the last time we saw each other?"

"That would be Manhattan, five years ago, when AC tried to have me killed for fucking his then fiancée," Bishop replied.

I didn't know what to think listening to their conversation. It was the next morning after we had took out Duke Carrington. It was a business day. Everybody was at work. Everybody except us. We were in an expensive hotel in Crystal City, the Arlington, Virginia area, about mile or so from the Pentagon. We had spent the night here and yes, we had explosive sex again—actually two times since checking the hotel.

The police found four men at Duke's Chesapeake home along with several women taking care of newborn babies. They also found several young girls waiting to deliver babies. So Detectives Rosenberg and Whitfield still ended up being heroes. Chris and the two women who had died a couple of nights ago were also found in Shakira's house and those murders were attributed to Duke as well.

Finally, I made a call back to the detectives and gave them Duke's whereabouts. Bishop had me tell them that the smart move would be to write it up as a gunfight between the detectives and Duke. Of course they jumped at that opportunity.

What's better for cops than being double heroes? That definitely beat a dozen of donuts and coffee.

I was my now Bishop's ride and die bitch.

UNIQUE

My future was bright and this was my new beginning.

"Bishop, go fuck yourself!" Anthony Carter said excitedly. I was sure he probably had the woman killed that Bishop fucked. I wonder why she did it and more importantly, why did he do it.

Bishop laughed at his comment. "I'm not going to prolong this communication," he began. "Family has always been off limits, but you brothers changed the game. You killed Neeko and he wasn't a threat to you guys operation. He was trying to go straight and never fucked with anyone, but you guys sanction Duke Carrington, and now, my brother is dead,"

"Bishop, it wasn't like that, and you know that," Terrence Carter replied. "We didn't have control over Carrington. He was a rogue. If anything, the pressure may have been on to pay us, but we didn't sanction anything."

"TC, AC, it was nice talking to you brothers again." The conversation went silent. Then Bishop broke the silence. "By the way, those things that go bump in the night, that's me!"

He hung up the phone and a new chapter was born.

Coming Soon

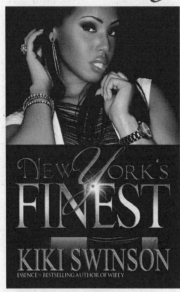

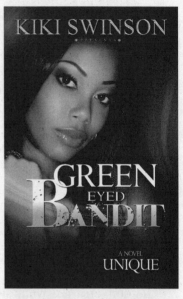

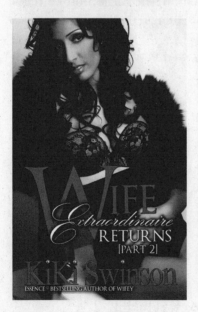

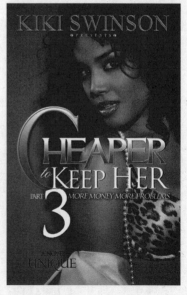